MONTROSE

By

Rhonda Braden

This book is a work of fiction. Places, events, and situations in this story are purely fictional. Any resemblance to actual persons, living or dead, is coincidental.

© 2002 by Rhonda Braden. All rights reserved.

No part of this book may be reproduced, stored in a retrieval system, or transmitted by any means, electronic, mechanical, photocopying, recording, or otherwise, without written permission from the author.

ISBN: 1-4033-7120-2 (e-book)
ISBN: 1-4033-7121-0 (Paperback)
ISBN: 1-4033-7122-9 (Dustjacket)

Library of Congress Control Number: 2002094244

This book is printed on acid free paper.

Printed in the United States of America
Bloomington, IN

1stBooks - rev. 12/10/02

IN MEMORY OF

This book is dedicated to the memory of my parents, John and Louise Buchanan, and to my niece and guardian angel, Amber D. Hayes.

ACKNOWLEDGEMENTS

I would like to thank my loving husband, Ron, for the encouragement given and patience shown, as I worked on this project. Special thanks, to my beautiful and insightful daughter, Brandy, who gave me confidence and to my lovely family for believing in me and lending support. Last but not the least, thanks to my friends – Janice, who was tremendously helpful with technical support and advice, and to Roberta, your encouraging words made all the difference in the world.

To all of you, who made a contribution in your special way, I say thanks. From my heart to yours, may God keep you always. I love you all!

CHAPTER I

THE ASSIGNMENT

Jade was sitting behind her desk with a pencil in her mouth searching the ads for an apartment, when she stopped momentarily. She picked up a cup of hot tea and sipped it, as she looked into the noisy newsroom – through the large glass window from inside her office.

Jade smiled as she watched the reporters, editors, copyboys and photographers scrambling around the room – banging on keyboards, talking and yelling at each other.

It was a busy and noisy place, but it was exciting to Jade – she loved her job.

Jade Lewis is a 26-year-old investigative newspaper reporter for the Nashville *Gazette.*

She has lived in Nashville, for the past three years.

Jade is a very attractive girl. She stands about five feet, four inches tall, has a caramel – colored complexion, light brown eyes and long, wavy golden brown hair. She is intelligent, articulate, independent and very aggressive.

Jade is originally from Chicago, and comes from a middle – class African American family, her father, Dr. John Lewis, was one of the most sought after heart surgeons in the country, yet he dedicated most of his practice to serving the poor and underprivileged in Cook County.

Jade, being an only child was the apple of his eye – and she adored her father.

Jade's mother Carol, is a retired schoolteacher. She is deeply involved in church activities and Social Charities.

As a young girl, Jade would often go with her father to his office. He had hoped she would develop an interest in the medical field, however, he noticed that his young daughter had other talents and interests in mind.

She had very good writing skills and an inquisitive mind. She would often ask his patients, as they sat in the waiting room, questions about their health conditions. The patients loved the

little girl, whose long pigtails hung down her back. They looked forward to answering her questions as she jotted down the information on one of her father's note pads.

This irritated Jade's mother, who wanted her daughter to be more interested in music, dance and the arts – but Jade detested those type of activities. Carol didn't think it was proper for Jade to be hanging around her husband's clinic, mingling with sick people.

Dr. Lewis would ignore most of his wife's nagging, as would Jade, which was constant and endless.

Jade's lease was going to be up by the end of the month, and she did not want to renew it. She needed more space and wanted to live closer to her job.

Jade had been contemplating purchasing a condominium, but she couldn't find the time to fit it into her schedule. The real estate market was red-hot and ripe for purchasing with low interest rates, however she had not taken the time to explore it. She promised herself she would look into it next year.

While scanning the paper, her eyes fell upon a listing for a large upstairs apartment, with a separate entrance, two bedrooms, kitchen, living room, washer/dryer hookup and one bath.

"Umm," sighed Jade. "This looks interesting."

The rent was only $800 per month, which was well within her budget. It was cheaper than where she was currently staying, and much larger.

***This is a steal,* she thought. She could use the second bedroom as an office – and since it had a washer/dryer connection, she would not have to go to the laundromat to do her clothes, which had been a nuisance.**

***Wonder where this is,* she thought. There was only a telephone number listed – but no address or contact name.**

Just as she was about to pick up the telephone, it rang. The noise startled her, then she picked up the receiver, "Jade Lewis," she said.

"Jade," the familiar voice on the other line said. "This is Sean. Can you come to my office? I need to speak with you."

"Okay, I'll be right there," Jade stated. *Well I guess I'll have to make this call later,* she thought, circling the ad, she left for her boss's office.

Jade attended Northwestern University, and graduated with honors in journalism.

In her sophomore year, her father had a heart attack and died. On his deathbed, he told Jade to follow her dreams and pursue a career in journalism. He realized long ago, his daughter would not follow in his footsteps and take up his profession.

Jade was a biology major at the time and had planned to pursue her studies in medicine however, after hearing her father's confession she changed her major to journalism. This was where her heart and true talents were.

At Northwestern she met, and became very good friends with her current boss, Sean Winslow. Sean was white and very attractive. He was from a prominent upper middle – class family in Nashville.

His great grandfather was founder and owner of the largest newspaper there, the *Gazette*. It had been handed down to Sean's

father, John Winslow; until his untimely death. Now his uncle Robert Winslow was the chief executive officer. Sean was next in line to inherit the business, since his uncle didn't have any children.

While at Northwestern, Jade and Sean worked together as reporters for the school newspaper. They shared a special kinship since they both had lost their fathers, whom they were very close to.

Sean had a crush on Jade, and thought she was the most beautiful girl he had ever seen. She would often tease him about his looks, calling him a poor little rich white boy who looked Latino because of his tanned skin and dark features. He reminded her of the actor Andy Garcia.

After graduation, Sean, who was a couple of years older than Jade, went home to work for his family's newspaper company. Jade went back to Chicago and worked for the Johnson's Publishing Company.

Several years later, Sean had become managing editor of the paper's investigative reporting division.

When a position became available in that section, he called and offered it to Jade – who was more than willing to accept it. They'd stayed in touch through e-mails and he knew how discouraged Jade was with her present job.

She wanted to get out of Chicago and away from her mother, who had become more than unbearable since the death of her father.

"I've got an assignment for you; maybe this will be something that will spark your creative talents." Sean said, as Jade walked into his cluttered office. She looked around the room where papers were scattered about, and covered the top of his desk. ***Neatness was not one of Sean's virtues,*** **Jade thought.**

"What is it Sean," Jade asked suspiciously. "The last time you gave me an assignment that 'sparked my talents,' – as you put it – I ended up embarrassing several of Bob's politician friends."

"Ooh yes – how well do I remember! We both almost lost our jobs, and if it wasn't for Bob we wouldn't be here today," Sean responded.

"Have you run this by him, has Bob given me the okay," Jade asked.

"Yeah, he has," replied Sean. "As a matter of fact he's the one who asked me to give it to you. He thought you'd be perfect for the job."

Jade sat straight up in her chair and in a surprised tone of voice asked, "What? You mean Bob recommended *me* for this job?"

"Yeah," replied Sean, and with a puzzling look on his face, he told her they both had a meeting with Bob in an hour.

"Have you any idea what this is all about, Sean?" Jade asked inquisitively.

"Well, all I know is that it's something about home equity fraud and scams." Sean shrugged and continued. "It must be something big, or really important to him. My uncle doesn't usually involve himself with the small – stuff and he normally doesn't get involved with giving out assignments."

***Predatory lending,* Jade thought. "This is strange. Do you know anybody who's been scammed lately? I mean; has there been anything in the news that would have prompted him to want**

to do a story? And why would he suggest me? Do you think he's trying to get back at me?"

"Stop it Jade," demanded Sean.

"Well, what do you think it is? And why does he want to see both of us Mr. Winslow? Doesn't that, spark your curiosity?" Jade asked and smiled as she stood up to leave.

Sean also stood up, and walked around his desk in front of Jade and said, "Maybe. You see Jade, my uncle knows that I will stand behind your decisions no matter what – and he probably knows that I can't say no to you."

Jade interrupted, "Sean, – you are a married man – and besides, I don't think the Winslows are ready to mess up their blue – blood lineage – or, as my mother would say – their, *pristine image* by having an African – American in-law."

They both laughed, and Sean leaned over to kiss Jade on the cheek.

"How's the apartment hunting coming along?" Sean asked.

"I think I may have found something, it really sounds like a good deal. I'm going now to call about it," said Jade as she walked out the door.

Sean called out, "Good luck – and don't forget about our meeting!"

Jade returned to her office. She immediately picked up the newspaper, where she had circled the ad, – and called the telephone number.

"Hello, this is Jade Lewis and I'm calling about your apartment ad, listed in today's paper."

"Who? Who did you say this is?" replied the voice on the other end of the telephone.

"Jade Lewis," she repeated. Jade noticed that the voice on the telephone was an elderly lady. "I'm calling about the apartment – is it still available?"

"Yes ma'am. It sure is. Would you like to come by to see it *today*? It's clean as a whistle," the elderly lady said, cheerfully. "My grandson lived up there, but he moved out to go – and shack up with that woman he calls his girlfriend. Chile, you ought to see her, – I look younger than she does," she laughed. "And honey – I'm seventy years old."

Jade couldn't help but smile to herself, and thought she sounded like a sweet little old lady.

"I won't be able to come by today. How about tomorrow at noon?" Jade asked.

"That will be all right, where do you work, baby? Are you single?" asked the elderly woman.

Jade replied, "I am a writer for the *Gazette* and yes I am single."

"Oh really, I bet you are a smart girl! Well, I'll see you tomorrow – and I'm going to fix you some lunch, okay?" The woman said, as she was about to hang up.

"How sweet of you Ms. – uh" Jade said, realizing that she didn't get her name.

"Mama Jo honey. Just call me Mama Jo," the friendly sounding woman said.

Jade didn't have the address – and hurriedly asked for it.

Mama Jo responded, "1275 Montrose Avenue."

As Jade hung up the telephone she couldn't help but feel a moment of nostalgia. The sweetness in Mama Jo's voice reminded her of one of her father's patients – Mrs. Fannie Mae Brown.

As she sat there reminiscing, the telephone rang, "Hey girl, what's up?" It was her girlfriend, Kim.

"Nothing girl, just sitting here – caught up in the moment," answered Jade.

"What's going on, have you found an apartment yet?" Kim asked.

Jade went on to tell her about the meeting with Sean and the one they scheduled with Bob. She also told her about the conversation with Mama Jo, and how nice she seemed to be.

"That sounds too good to be true. All that for just $800, are you sure? You don't think it's in bad shape, do you? Something must be wrong with it. And did you say something about lunch? Girl, pick me up tomorrow – I'm going with you!

"I bet she can cook! You know old people can get down on some food – and besides, you need somebody there to watch your back, girl. You just don't go waltzing up into some neighborhood you don't know nothing about. Oops – I forgot I was talking to the super sleuth investigator – Ms. Angela Lansbury," chided Kim.

"Girlfriend, between the time I hang up this telephone, and the time I pick you up tomorrow, you will have called everybody you know in Nashville, and have the 411 about Montrose Avenue – Ms. Snoop Dog," Jade said, as she laughed and looked at her watch. "Gotta go girlfriend, time for my meeting, I'll call you tonight."

Bob's office was on the sixth floor, three fights up from Jade's office. Normally, she would have taken the stairs – she enjoyed the exercise. Today, she decided to take the elevator – she didn't want to appear rushed.

"Good morning, Ms. Smith," Jade said cheerfully.

"Good morning to you, Jade," Bob's administrative assistant said, "Mr. Winslow is expecting you."

"Come on in Jade and have a seat. Would you like something to drink?" Bob asked, as Jade walked into his office.

She looked over at Sean, who was sipping on a bottle of spring water.

"I'll have a bottle of water, thank you," replied Jade.

As she sat down, she couldn't help but notice how well Bob kept himself for a man in his late fifties. He was about five – eleven, and had very broad shoulders narrowing down to a trim waistline. He had salt and pepper gray hair, and his complexion was the same color as Sean's.

He was a very attractive man. Bob, as Mr. Winslow was called by most people at the company, was very professional. He was a stern looking man, with a bit of arrogance about him.

Yet, Sean once told her, that underneath that intimidating exterior – he really was a gentle man, full of insecurities. Bob always felt that his father had more confidence in Sean's father – who he thought would be better at running the business.

"Well Jade and Sean – I guess I've kept you in suspense long enough," Bob said, as he handed Jade a cup and a bottle of water.

He continued to stand as he spoke. "I guess what I'm trying to say is that there is more to this assignment than meets the eye. I more or less have a personal interest, and what I'm about to tell you is going to be very – very – private."

Bob appeared nervous. As he sat down behind his desk, he cleared his throat, and his voice deepened. "I personally chose

you, Jade, because I trust you. I respect your work, your professionalism, and your integrity. You are one of the best reporters we have."

"Thank you sir," smiled Jade.

"I have been watching you for a long time, and your work is good. You have developed quite a following among our readers. I like that." Bob paused, and leaned forward onto his desk.

He looked at both Sean and Jade, and said, "Look, I know that I came down hard on the both of you during the First General Bank story, but it had gotten out of hand – especially when a couple of our politicians were implicated.

"But Jade, I have to give it to you. Young lady you showed true grit, even if it meant jeopardizing your job, and for that I could have never fired you. It's your do or die attitude I admire.

"As for you nephew – you believed in her. And you had the guts to stand steadfast in her defense. I admire that also," his voice trailed, and then softened. "I'm proud of you son. You remind me of your Father. Your strength, your vision, and your wisdom."

At that moment, Sean felt a sense of sadness for his uncle. It was as if Bob was remembering what his father had seen in Sean's father and not in him.

Sean looked up at his uncle, and said in a solemn voice, "I remind myself of you Bob. You see, I never got the chance to work with my father. All that I have left of him are memories. You're the motivation behind me. I've watched and learned from you."

Although Jade was proud of the way Sean responded to Bob, she felt uncomfortable in this setting. She knew that she would soon begin to think about her father.

So in a light-hearted manner, Jade interrupted, "If you all keep this up, you're going to make me cry."

Both feeling a little embarrassed, Bob and Sean looked over at Jade, and apologized. Bob cleared his throat, and proceeded to pick up the conversation where he'd left off.

"As I was saying, Jade, I want you to look into home equity frauds and renovation scams."

Bob handed Jade and Sean a stack of papers. "Here is some information from the Federal Trade Commission and other

newspaper articles about some local cases. This should be enough to get you started."

Jade and Sean listened intently, as Bob continued. "Generally older homeowners are popular targets of fraudulent home repair financing schemes. They're likely to live in older homes that need repair; they've built up substantial equity, and are less likely to do the work themselves.

"These lenders don't care about the borrower's ability to pay, so long as they have enough home equity to secure the new loan. The lenders are able to prey on elderly and poor homeowners because mortgage transactions are often very complicated, and difficult to understand."

"Isn't this illegal? And what about the FTC – are they aware of these practices?" Jade asked.

"I hate to say it, Jade, but it's legal, Bob said sadly. And as long as the lenders can get the people to sign the contract, it's binding. And yes, the Federal Trade Commission is aware of these practices, and they will handle any complaint that comes through their offices about shoddy or incomplete work. But the loans – unless obtained illegally – stand.

Jade immediately thought about Mrs. Fannie Mae Brown or Mr. DeAngelo, and the majority of her father's patients. They were all elderly, low-income, and minority. They would be easy prey for these people.

Jade, like her father, had much compassion for the poor and elderly.

Sean, knowing how compassionate, and sensitive Jade is about people – sensed her emotions, and interrupted her thoughts. "Jade, we will have to set some boundaries here, I don't believe Bob is talking about you bringing down the entire FTC with this investigation."

He and Bob broke out into laughter. Sean was joking and wanted to make her laugh – but Jade wasn't feeling it.

"What would be wrong with that? Ethics and moral issues should be just as important as illegalities!" Jade said.

Bob was leaning back in his chair, but sensed Jade's annoyance, he sat up and explained, "No, no, Jade, we aren't going in that direction. See, all I want to do is rock the boat a little. To exploit and expose. That alone should cause uproar with

the consumer groups – and hopefully would be enough to get the attention of the federal government.

"There's one article I just gave you. I especially want you to read and familiarize yourself with it. It's about a middle-aged white man named Lester Albright who owned a mortgage company. Making home equity loans to higher-risk borrowers was his specialty.

"He had scammed a lot of families in the Waverly Park community, and over a period of time, he ended up owning a lot of their property. He was quite a charmer and a smooth talker."

Bob paused, then shook his head and said, "Of all the stories that I had heard – and believe me, they were all sad, – but one of the saddest, was when he foreclosed on a home owned by an elderly black couple he had befriended.

"He convinced them to take out a loan because their house needed some repairs. They were both in their late eighties, on fixed incomes, and had very little savings. They had bought the house, and had been living there since1954.

"After they realized that they could not continue to make these high – interest payments, Albright foreclosed on their loan.

Since the couple had no other relatives, Albright had power of attorney over their affairs, and he forced them into a nursing home.

"They were devastated, and both died shortly thereafter – on the same day, an hour apart."

Jade and Sean sat in awe. She'd decided not to blow up like she had earlier, but underneath her pensive look, she was salivating.

Jade thirsted for this story. She wasn't sure why, but she was definitely feeling it.

After a moment of silence, Bob continued, "Lester, being the unsavory character he was, had the nerve to tear down their home, and build himself a brand – new, all brick, three – bedroom, ranch – style house on that very property. It really looked out of place in that neighborhood."

"Why would he want to live in the same neighborhood where he steals and cheats from the people?" asked Sean.

"I don't know," answered Bob. "But I do know the residents became infuriated with him because of the shoddy repair work, on their houses, and what he did to the little old couple. One year

later the residents banned together through their community association, hired an attorney and brought a civil action lawsuit, for breach of contract and conversion, against him."

"Oh really," Jade said, with excitement in her voice. "Did they follow through with it?"

Bob responded, "Hold on Jade, this story gets better, well, in some ways it does. You see, the association filed the lawsuit against him, however on the morning he was due in court, Mr. Albright was found dead in his car parked in front of his house, he had been shot twice in the chest. To this day, the murder remains unsolved."

At that moment Bob's administrative assistant buzzed in, "Excuse me, Mr. Winslow; don't forget you have a meeting in about fifteen minutes."

"Thank you, Ms. Smith, I lost track of the time." Bob said.

Jade sat in disbelief. She couldn't wait to get her hands on Lester Albright, but someone else had already killed him.

At that point she was puzzled. *So why would he still be an issue if he was dead? Did Bob want her to find out who killed him?*

Earlier Bob had said something about this being personal or private – what did he mean? **She was very confused.**

Bob interrupted her thoughts and said, "I've got to hurry and wrap this up. Needless to say, the lawsuit was eventually dropped by the association because of other litigation against Albright's estate. It will be tied up in court for years.

"Someone, under an assumed business name – a blind partner, or something – has taken over the business and has picked up, it appears, where Lester Albright left off.

"I can't figure it out. That's where you come in Jade. I need you to investigate and find out who it is. Find out also who bought that house – it could be a start.

"Now, as I had mentioned earlier, the reason I have a personal interest in this matter is because – Bob stopped, again he appeared nervous. He looked at Sean who was staring back at his uncle with fear and apprehension.

"What is it Bob?" Sean asked. Bob stood up, walked over to his window, and began to speak. "About twenty – something years ago, I had an affair with a nurse who was taking care of

mother when she became sick and bedridden. Her name was Nikki.

"She was very special to me. She was a very pretty girl, and we fell in love. This relationship continued for about two years, until my wife found out about it.

"She was devastated and went to my father – threatening to divorce me if I didn't stop seeing Nikki. My father was disappointed, and forbade me to ever see her again.

"Nikki was a single parent and a very good mother to her two – year – old son. They lived with her parents.

"One day Nikki asked me for a $5,000 loan. She told me it was to pay off a high-interest loan her parents had made for home repairs.

"She was upset that day, and said someone name Lester Albright was threatening to take her parent's house if they didn't pay the loan up.

"I was leaving town the next day, and I told her I would take care of it when I got back. After I returned, my wife confronted me about the affair, and I learned my father had fired Nikki. I

tried my best to get in touch with her – but I never could. She wouldn't return my calls.

"I never saw her again, but I had heard she had started working for the same man that was trying to take her parents home. Three years later, my mother – who had been very fond of Nikki – called me to her bedside. She told me that Peggy, the nurse who had replaced Nikki, knew her, and said that Nikki had committed suicide.

"I was heartbroken and shocked with the news and so was my mother. She told me that Nikki had two children, and that she felt sorry for them. I told Mother she only had a son, but Peggy had informed her that Nikki had a two-year-old daughter also.

Bob's voice softened, and with a painful look on his face, he said, "At that point I was even more confused, wondering if that child was mine. Mother, through instinct or intuition must have read my mind. She also had her suspicions. She told me that she had sent $1,000 for each child anonymously to the family, and suggested I leave it at that.

"Mother convinced me it would only create a scandal, and cause the family shame if I pursued it. You see, mother knew that

we had been seeing each other but she never let on, I think deep in her heart, she was okay with it."

Bob was still standing and looking out of the window when Sean asked, "What was so shameful about finding out the truth? Didn't you want to know if she was your daughter?"

Bob turned to Sean with a forlorn look on his face, he sighed and said, "Sean, Nikki was Black."

Jade was in awe of what she had just heard. There were so many questions running through her mind, but she felt awkward and didn't know if she should say anything.

She looked at Sean who looked straight ahead. Jade couldn't feel him, but she knew he was in deep thought about what he had just heard.

"I'm sorry to have to tell you this son," Bob said. "But I've lived with the secret guilt far too long. I realize I should have done something about this a long time ago, but I didn't. I feel shame for allowing myself to be talked out of pursuing this matter, and owning up to my responsibility. I've prayed so many times, asking for forgiveness – especially if that child is my daughter. If she is mine, I want to know, I need to know."

Bob sat back down in his chair. Jade saw he seemed to have aged in these past few moments. He also appeared relieved and at peace.

"I think you've made the right decision Bob," Jade reluctantly said.

"Thanks Jade, and I apologize to you also – but please know I wasn't just using Nikki. She meant more to me than you could ever know," Bob paused a second, then continued.

"I don't know why, but something tells me Albright had something to do with Nikki's suicide. Whoever is running that business now is somehow involved also. I can't do anything to Lester. He got what he deserved, but I sure as hell can destroy what's left of his rotten business, and destroy anybody else connected with it."

Bob looked at Jade as if he needed her approval, and asked, "Now do you understand? Do you think that you'll be able to handle this, Jade?"

Jade, was unsure of what she could handle, but she knew she wanted this story. She looked at Bob, and said with as much

confidence as she could, "Yes sir, I do understand. I'll get started on it right away."

As she stood up to shake Bob's hand, she reassured him she wouldn't disappoint him.

"I know you won't – that's why I chose you Jade." Bob said as he picked up his attaché case.

Sean, who had been sitting very quietly, stood and shook his uncle's hand, he held it for a moment, then said, "I'm very proud of you uncle Bob. Everyone makes mistakes, but it takes a real man to admit to them – and a courageous one who will try to change them."

Bob hugged his nephew, and said, "Thanks for being so understanding."

As Jade witnessed this moment, she thought how special Sean was. He was never judgmental of people, and saw them for who they were. She was glad they were friends, and glad to be working for him.

Before she walked out of the door, she asked, "Oh yeah Bob, where is this house Lester Albright built?"

Bob shuffled some papers on his desk, and replied as he picked up a note, "I think it's on Montrose Avenue. Yes that's it, Montrose."

"*Montrose?*" Jade called out. "That's the same street the apartment I'm going to look at tomorrow is on."

"*Really?*" Bob and Sean said at the same time.

"I'll tell you what, if you like that apartment, we'll pay the rent as long as you are on this assignment," Bob said.

***"Cool,"* Jade said, and gave a thumbs – up to Sean as she was leaving the Office.**

On the way to her office, Jade was thinking about the meeting, she just left.

The revelations were mystifying, suspenseful and intriguing to her. She felt compelled to accept this assignment, though she wasn't sure why she felt this way. She just knew it was something that she had to do.

But unbeknownst to Jade, Sean or Mr. Winslow, this assignment would prove to be a catalysts that would open the doors to a floodgate of secrets that will ultimately affect their lives – and the lives of others – forever.

Montrose

by **Rhonda Braden**

ISBN **1-4033-7121-0**
(softcover)
ISBN **1-4033-7122-9**
(hardcover)

"Montrose," is a powerfully charged mystery/romance novel, with a plot thickened by many surprise twists and turns from the beginning to the end. The Author brilliantly evokes an array of heartfelt emotions, and passion from each of the characters in the book.

The main character, an investigative newspaper reporter, feels compelled to take on an assignment offered by her editor. The revelations are mystifying, suspenseful, and intriguing. However, this assignment will prove to be a very dangerous feat for her.

Available from
1st Books Library

To order call
~~**1-888-280-7715**~~
or visit
www.montrosebook.com

Montrose

by Rhonda Braden

ISBN 1-4033-7121-0
(softcover)
ISBN 1-4033-7122-9
(hardcover)

"Montrose, a powerfully charged mystery/romance novel.

**Available from
1st Books Library**

To order call
1-888-280-7715
or visit
www.montrosebook.com

CHAPTER II

MONTROSE

Montrose was on the south side of town, in the Waverly Park Community Neighborhood. It turns off onto 12th Street, and is a well – traveled thoroughfare.

This urban neighborhood is between downtown, and the popular Vanderbilt Village. It is a neighborhood commercial village of specialty shops and multi-ethnic restaurants. A stable middle – income area, Waverly Park is dominated by 1920's to 1940's homes.

A large percentage of the homes have been renovated since the early Seventies, but the neighborhood still offers opportunities for owner-occupant renovators.

***This area doesn't sound too bad,* thought Jade as she closed the magazine called Nashville Neighborhoods. She telephoned Kim to**

let her know that she was on the way to pick her up. She made a few more calls and then left.

Earlier that morning, she and Sean had met for coffee in the cafeteria to lay out the plan for her new assignment – and to also discuss Bob's secret.

Jade wanted to make sure Sean was okay, since she didn't get a chance to talk with him after their meeting with Bob. He reassured her that he was alright, even though he was still trying to process everything, he heard.

"The man is human, he wants to right a wrong," Sean said.

He was more upset and embarrassed by how his family had reacted than anything. They were more concerned about their own reputations than finding out the true identity of an innocent child.

Sean thought this was probably the reason for the problem between his grandfather and uncle-and also the reason why Bob's wife constantly drank and remained aloof from the rest of the family.

However, Bob bore the guilt; his past had haunted him for all these years.

Bob had spent years wondering why this woman would commit suicide, or what would drive her to that point. Bob had so much to deal with, that Sean really felt sorry for him, and wanted to help him out as much as he could.

Jade wanted to help also, and reassured Sean, she would do her very best.

"Jade, I really appreciate your understanding, sorry you have to be dragged into my family's secret affairs," Sean said.

"See – I tried to tell you Sean. Your family would not allow their blue – blood lineage to be disturbed. If we had gotten married, they would have disowned you. There's no telling what would have happened if we had some little mixed breeds running around," Jade said, jokingly.

They both laughed. "I wouldn't have cared about what they were feeling, as long as I had you, I would have been the happiest man in the world," Sean said affectionately.

Jade felt honored, "That is so sweet of you Sean, I appreciate that, but it's too bad destiny had other plans for us. Sorry."

Jade was glad to see that Sean was alright and in a better mood. He was her friend and she really cared.

Jade drove into the parking lot of the office building where Kim worked. Kim was walking out of the door, when she spotted Jade.

"Hey girl, what's going on?" Kim asked as she got into Jade's 2000 fiery red Toyota Celica.

"Nothing much, just trying to keep it real," Jade responded as she hugged her girlfriend.

Kim, was a tall, slim and attractive girl. She was very stylish and creative when it came to her hair and clothing. Jade had met Kim shortly after she moved to Nashville three years ago, at the wedding shower of a mutual friend.

She liked Kim's sassiness, her friendly, out going personality, and confident "in your face, speak your mind" attitude.

Kim was responsible for Jade's make-over. She would tease her about looking like a preppy nerd from the north. Jade, taking her friend's advice cut her long wavy ponytail to a neck length curly twists style and she started to dress more fashionably.

Jade filled Kim in on what was going on. As they drove down 12th Street toward the Waverly Park neighborhood, Kim noticed her friend was quiet and preoccupied. "You okay?" she asked.

Jade looked over at her friend and answered, "Kim, I hope I haven't bitten off more than I can chew. This is some deep stuff, and I don't want to let Sean and Bob down, I want to do a good job."

"So what's stopping you?" Kim asked.

With frustration in her voice, Jade said, "Well, we are talking about a mysterious murder, a suicide, the paternity of a twenty – something girl, who I don't even know if she still exists. Then there are exposing sleazy business practices along with the sleazy owners, and lord only knows what else could come up. I don't have a clue as to who, what, or where to start."

"Girl, I don't believe what I'm hearing. You were made for this kind of story!" Kim exclaimed. "This is classic Jade. It's what you do best, sweetheart. Bob and Sean knows it, they have faith in you, and so do I. So stop tripping."

Kim said it convincingly – but in her heart, she too, was nervous about this assignment. She thought about how dangerous it could be for Jade.

"Thanks for your vote of confidence, Kim," Jade said. "Once this apartment hunt is over and I get settled in, I will be able to put things in prospective and be a little more focused.

"I suppose I could start by contacting some of the members of the community association – since they filed the lawsuit against Albright. There might be someone in the neighborhood willing to help me out.

"Anyway, I read about this neighborhood in a magazine and it really sounds like a nice area," Jade said, as she was trying to convince herself that everything would be okay.

"Well, I've got something better than that, Kim said. "Do you remember my girl Tee?"

"You mean the girl who dances at the strip club?" Jade asked.

"Yeah, that's the one – but she doesn't dance anymore. Tee cleaned up her act, and met some man who opened up a hair salon in the Village for her. You know, girlfriend could always hook a sistah' up with some hairdos.

"Well, I called her yesterday, and told her you would be calling for an appointment. Also, you were writing a story about the Waverly Park neighborhood and needed her help. She grew up in that area. I asked her about Lester Albright, and she said she knew the scumbag – she's ready to tell you whatever you needed to know! She's at T's Urban Reflection hair salon. Here's the number – call her."

Jade smiled as she responded to her friend, "See Kim, what did I tell you yesterday. I knew by the time I picked you up, you would have the hook-up for me girlfriend. You are too much, but you are alright with me."

Kim, in her animated state, rocked her head from side to side, and snapped her fingers to a Mary J. Blige CD that was playing, said to Jade, "I told you girl – ***I got your back."***

They both laughed as Jade drove down 12th Street and turned left onto Montrose Avenue. She pulled in front of the address, and they both got out of the car.

"Jade was impressed at how well kept these older homes were, and how nice the manicured lawns looked. Mama Jo lived in a

two – story red brick house lined with shrubbery. It had a big oak tree in the yard.

The stairwell to the upstairs apartment was white wrought iron, and matched the white trimming around the windows and frame of the house. She had a front porch that extended the entire length of the house, and a white porch swing.

Kim looked at Jade, and raised her hand for a high five. She said, "Girlfriend, this is nice! Wonder what it looks like on the inside?"

"We'll know in a minute – but if it's anything like the outside, it's got to be nice," Jade responded.

Just as they were approaching the two steps onto the porch, the front door opened and there stood a medium – height, slightly overweight woman with a scarf tied around her head.

The round – faced lady, with high cheekbones had a beautiful wide smile, and shiny white teeth. Jade immediately felt a sense of comfort towards her.

"Come on in girls, I'm Josephine Johnson, but call me Mama Jo. Now which one of you pretty girls is Ms. Jade?" she asked, as they stepped inside.

Jade reached out to shake her hand, and said, "I am. I'm Jade Lewis and this is my girlfriend Kim Murphy."

"Hello Mama Jo," Kim said, as she extended her hand. "I hope you don't mind that I tagged along, Jade wasn't sure where this area was, and I was somewhat familiar."

"Oh Chile, that's fine, I love company – the more the merrier. Come on to the table, I know you girls are hungry, and we can talk there," Mama Jo said as she led them into her dining room.

As they walked through the house the girls were impressed with how neat and clean it was. Mama Jo had Queen Anne furniture in the living room and more contemporary furniture in the den. Along one wall stood a huge solid wood entertainment center with a big – screen color television, a VCR, and a nice sound system. Two large speakers were recessed in the other cubicles.

There were video tapes neatly stacked on one side, and CDs stacked on the other.

Individual and family photos were also displayed on the ledges and tables all over the house.

The dining room had a large cherry wood table that sat six and it was covered with an off – white lace tablecloth. Along the wall stood a china cabinet filled with old, but beautiful china.

"Do you live alone, Mama Jo? I don't mean to pry but I noticed that you had a big collection of video tapes and CD's in the den," Jade asked as she and Kim sat down at the table.

Mama Jo, who had an infectious smile and laugh, said, "Chile, you don't think Mama Jo like movies and music?"

"No ma'am, it's not that," said Jade, wishing that she had never asked that question.

As Mama Jo was busy placing food on the table, she explained that her granddaughter lived with her and she reminded Jade that her grandson had just moved out.

Mama Jo had prepared lasagna, a large salad and a freshly baked pecan pie. She also placed a pitcher of iced tea on the table, and the look and smell of the food made Jade and Kim very hungry.

"Do you cook like this everyday for lunch?" asked Kim.

Mama Jo responded, "No baby, not everyday. Only when I'm having company. Most of the time, I'll have leftovers from the

night before. Sometimes my son and grandson come here for lunch, and I'll whip up something for them.

"Honey, Mama Jo just loves to cook," she said cheerfully.

"Jennifer, my granddaughter has funny eating ways, that girl don't like nothing. She ain't big as a bird. I hope you get to meet her and my son. He said he would try to come by for lunch. He's a detective you know, and chile, Tom was sure proud of him when he graduated from the police academy." Mama Jo said as she shook her head with this faraway look in her eyes.

"Is Tom your husband?" Jade asked.

Mama Jo looked at Jade, and smiled, "Yes baby. But he's dead now, he's resting. It's been two years and I sure do miss him. We were married for forty five years."

"Wow, that's a long time! Hope I can find somebody to marry me, I'll be happy if we stayed together *ten* years," Kim said, as she laughed.

"Chile, don't you sell yourself short like that. Neither one of you. You are too smart for that. You make a man respect you. Tell him what you want – and if he ain't giving it, let him go on and you find somebody else.

"Don't let no man use you. If it don't feel good to ya' then he ain't no good for ya," Mama Jo said defiantly.

This amused Jade and Kim. They gave each other high fives, as they sat at the table, enjoying Mama Jo's conversation.

Then Kim said, "I hear ya' Mama Jo, you my kind' a girl, and I like the way you think."

"Now that's what I'm talking about," added Jade.

Mama Jo laughed also. She was enjoying talking to these young girls, and she secretly hoped that Jade would like the apartment and rent it. She liked Jade, already.

Mama Jo blessed the food and everyone started to eat, the girls complimented her on how good everything was.

"Mama Jo, I haven't eaten this good since I went home last year for Thanksgiving" Jade said.

"Man, I don't think I've ever eaten this good – can I get seconds?" Kim asked playfully.

They all fell into laughter, and Mama Jo told them to eat as much as they wanted.

"Where are you girls from?" Mama Jo asked.

"I'm from Chicago, and I have been here for three years, working at the Gazette," Jade answered.

"I'm from here Mama Jo, I grew up in East Nashville," added Kim.

After they finished eating, the girls helped to clean off the table, and offered to put up the food.

"Don't worry about this mess. My son will be here to eat soon," Mama Jo said.

"Now I want you to go on upstairs and look at the apartment Jade. I sure hope you like it," she handed her the keys. "I would go, but I can't climb those steps."

Jade and Kim went upstairs. It was larger than Jade had imagined. It had been freshly painted, and was very clean.

Jade liked it, and she liked Mama Jo. It was perfect, she told Kim.

The second bedroom was large enough for an office. She could put a daybed in the room, so when her mother visited, she could sleep in there.

Mama Jo is not charging enough rent, I'll offer her more. It's worth it, and she could probably use the extra money for food,

medicine or whatever. I'll ask if I could move in this weekend too, **Jade thought.**

Kim thought it was perfect also, and wished she had spotted it first. As they left the apartment, they noticed a different car parked behind Jade's, and thought it might belong to Mama Jo's son.

Mama Jo was standing in the door as they approached, and asked, "Well baby, what you think? Do you like it?"

As they walked into Mama Jo's house, Jade hugged her and said, "Yes I do. I love it – and if it's alright with you, I would like to move in this weekend."

"That'll be fine with me, sugar," Mama Jo said.

Jade began to pull her checkbook out of her purse, and said, "Mama Jo, I am willing to pay more rent. I don't think you are charging enough. And what about a deposit?"

Just then a deep voice from out of nowhere chimed in. "She ***definitely*** **gets the apartment Mama, – and charge her $1,000, since she wants to pay more rent."**

Mama Jo was beaming with delight as she said, "Hush boy, I don't need a whole lot of money. This house is paid for, and I get

your daddy's pension. I don't have any bills, so Jade, bless your sweet little heart, thanks for the offer but $800 will be fine. And don't you worry about paying no deposit."

"Are you sure Mama Jo, let me at least pay a deposit," Jade asked."

"Chile, what did I just tell you?" Mama Jo asked, as she placed her hands on her hips and smiled.

"Okay – okay, Mama Jo. I heard you," Jade said, playfully and handed her a check for $1,600 to cover two month's rent.

"Phillip, come in here and meet these two pretty girls." Mama Jo said, as she leaned over and whispered, excitedly, "He's single and available you know. Thirty five years old, and got his own house too.

"But he works too much, and I tell him all the time he needs to slow down and find a wife," then she chuckled.

As Phillip walked into the room, he apologized for having food in his mouth. Jade and Kim noticed how handsome he was. Phillip was more than six feet tall, with pecan brown skin, and dark features. His black hair was cut short, and he had shiny white teeth – with a smile just like Mama Jo's.

"Good afternoon ladies," Phillip said, with a deep voice.

"Hello," Jade and Kim said respectively.

"Who's the young lady that doesn't think Mama is charging enough rent?" Phillip asked.

Jade raised her hand slightly and smiled.

Kim feeling flirty spoke up and said, "This is Jade Lewis, and I'm Kim Murphy, her friend." And then she blurted out, "I'm sorry but man, you are one *fine brother!*"

Everyone laughed and Kim's outburst seemed to have loosened Jade up a little.

She extended her hand to Phillip, and said, "You have the sweetest mother, and I didn't want to feel like I was taking advantage of her. I thought, she should charge more for the apartment. It's worth it, and I'm willing to pay more."

Phillip was still holding her hand when she noticed how strong, yet gentle his grasp was.

As Jade managed to pull her hand away, Phillip responded, "It's nice of you to feel that way, Jade. It says a lot about you. But I don't think you are going to be able to change Mama's mind."

"He's right, Jade – and I don't want to hear another word. See Phillip, I told you she was special. Jade, when I heard your voice over the telephone, something told me that you were the one I needed to rent the apartment to. Plenty of people called, but I just didn't feel good about them. So I asked God to help me out – and chile – He won't let you down! He let me know it was you, all you have to do is trust and believe in him honey, trust and believe!

When Jade and Kim got into the car to leave, all Kim could talk about was Phillip. She asked Jade, "Girl, did you see that tall, lean, chocolate dream?"

Jade responded, "I thought I would pass out when he held my hand." Mimicking Mama Jo's voice, she said, "And chile – I couldn't move! All I could do was raise my hand and smile."

They both laughed and gave each other high five's as they drove off listening to the soulful sounds of Mary J. Blige.

CHAPTER III

FOCUSING…

As Mama Jo's words rang out in Jade's mind, "All you have to do is trust and believe in Him, honey – trust and believe," suddenly she felt empowered. Jade had found a new sense of purpose. She could see her way. She was energized. The doubts and fears she felt earlier, no longer existed.

She knew what direction she'd take, and she chartered her path. She was focused and ready to take on this mission with a passion. She was hell – bent, and determined to expose the remnants of Lester Albright's past.

That's the least she could do for all the people he had scammed – and for the unsuspecting elderly couple he had stolen from.

She would uncover Nikki's suicide and find out if the daughter she had conceived was Bob's child. She could do that for

a man, who wanted to correct his past, and trusted and believed in her abilities enough to do the job.

As far as who killed Lester Albright was concerned, she could care less. She thought they deserved a medal – but curiosity got the best of her. She decided she would look into his murder – and if she ever found out who did it, she would never report it.

She just needed to know!

When Jade returned to her office, she informed Sean and Bob, she had accepted the apartment, and would be moving in that weekend. Bob was excited about Jade living in the neighborhood. He felt she would be able to gain the trust of the residents. They would be more likely to open up to her since she was living right there – as opposed to someone who just showed up for a story.

He asked Sean and Jade to get together and give him an outline of Jade's plans. He wanted to be informed, but he did not want to get in her way.

The next morning, Sean walked into Jade's office as she was gathering items she would need to set up in her home office. It had been decided that it would be easier for her to work from

home, and to only come into the office once a week to give a progress report.

"Knock, Knock" Sean said, pretending to knock on her open door. "Were you busy?"

Jade looked up and said, "No, no, come on in, I was just packing up a few things that I may need at home, I think I have everything now. Are you ready to go over my schedule with me? Here's your copy, and here's a copy for Bob. Would you mind giving this to him?"

Jade handed him two copies of outlines that had been neatly typed, and placed into clear portfolio folders.

Sean scanned his copy, and responded, "Jade – I'm impressed. This is so professional looking. When did you have the time to do it?"

"Have you forgotten, Sean that I am a professional – and you just have to make time for things that are important to you? Are there any questions or comments?" Jade asked sarcastically.

"No, there aren't any questions or comments. It looks good Jade – it really does, he said. "I guess you didn't need my

assistance. But that's nothing unusual. You never do. You always take care of your business."

In a more serious tone, he stated, "Jade, there is something I want to talk to you about."

"What is it Sean?" Jade asked quizzically.

Sean responded, "I have to admit I have some concerns about your well – being. There is some potential danger here. Don't get in too deep, Jade. Please know that at anytime you feel overwhelmed, pressured – if you fear for your life-be a wise girl, and pull out. I couldn't live with myself if anything happened to you."

Jade looked at Sean admirably, and said, "That's so sweet of you Sean, but listen, 'A wise man feareth, and departeth from evil: but the fool rageth, and is confident.' What I mean is, a wise man is cautious, and avoids danger. A fool plunges ahead with great confidence. Yes, I want to do a good job Sean, but I'm not going to compromise my life trying. I am confident – but I'm no fool. If this assignment becomes too much for me to handle, trust me – I'll be the first to let you know.

"Read the material. It's all outlined in there, I know there will be some deviations, but I won't know about those crossroads until I come upon them. That's what I was doing all last night – strategizing and planning how best to go about this investigation."

Sean nodded his head in agreement. He looked down at the report, and then back at Jade as she continued. "After I left you and Bob at the meeting yesterday, to be honest with you, I was very apprehensive about this assignment. I let doubt and fear cloud my judgment. However, after reflecting on something Mama Jo had said to me, my doubts and fears dissipated, I could actually see things a little clearer."

Sean looked at Jade and asked, "Why do I believe you?

"Oh, before I forget. Scooter has been assigned as your photographer. He's already been briefed –so give him a call."

"Scooter – the – shooter, I've seen his work, he's good. I'll give him a call," Jade replied.

After Sean left the office, and Jade had finished gathering her supplies, she decided to call her mother to fill her in on what was happening.

"Hello, Mother. This is Jade. How are you?" Jade asked, as she braced herself for the roller coaster ride that she knew she was about to embark on with her mother.

"Hi sweetheart, I'm fine. How are you doing? I was going to give you a call this weekend. I've really had you on my mind lately – is everything all right?" Mrs. Lewis asked.

"Everything is fine, Mother. I just wanted to call and let you know about the good things that are happening with me right now," Jade said cautiously.

"Oh really? Are you getting married? Did you get a promotion? Oh – I know what it is! You bought a condominium," Mrs. Lewis said, excited.

Jade sighed, and said, "None of those things, Mom. I've got this very exciting story I'm working on, and I've found this nice apartment. I will be moving this weekend, and I just wanted to share it with you."

Jade explained everything to her mother about the assignment, her new apartment, and the coincidence of it being in the same area that she would be working. As Jade suspected, this did not go over well with her mother.

"Jade, do you realize how dangerous this could be? If Mr. Winslow wants to find his daughter, then tell him to hire a private investigator. That's what this is all about – he's not concerned about poor people getting scammed.

"That happens on a daily basis. He just wants to put you out there to snoop into other people's lives so that you can do what he has neglected to do for the past twenty – some odd years. Jade, I'm your mother – and I am telling you right now, that you are forbidden to accept this job. If you would allow me, I'll call him and tell him so.

"What kind of neighborhood is he moving you into anyway? You don't need to rent an apartment. Your father left you more than enough money for you to purchase a house or condominium."

Jade rolled her eyes upward, sighed heavily, and said, "Mother, listen to me. I am 26 years old, and very capable of taking care of myself, making my own decisions, making choices on my job, speaking up for myself, and choosing where I live.

"As a matter of fact, I found the apartment myself; I researched the area before I even went there. I liked what I read about it – and now that I have seen it, I like it even more.

"It is a beautiful neighborhood, the apartment is huge, and it is a very safe place to live – and the landlord is a wonderful, God-fearing woman. Mother, I love this place. I'll live there for a year, and then I'll start looking for a house or condo."

Mrs. Lewis, realizing that she had angered her daughter, spoke in a more humbling tone, "Sweetheart, I know you are capable of making your own decisions. You are a very smart and independent young woman – and I am so proud of you. Nevertheless, sometimes our decisions can become clouded by all kinds of external factors.

"You are proud of yourself because your efforts have been acknowledged by the CEO of the company – who is obviously impressed with your work, and that's good. You are eager to do a good job because you know you are capable and daring – and this is certainly a challenge for you. Therefore, you want to prove yourself even more.

You've always had compassion for those who had been taken advantaged of, and you are dying to tell their story. Jade, honey, I realize how important all of these things are to you but there is a bigger picture here you are not seeing."

"Oh really Mom, just what is the big picture that I'm obviously not seeing?" Jade asked, sarcastically.

Mrs. Lewis responded, "Well, first of all, it's dangerous. You just can't go out there, hunt these people down, and bring them to justice."

Jade interrupted. She had heard enough. She knew her mother would go on and on – until she convinced her daughter to see things her way. "Mother, there is danger in everyday living. Trust me, I understand your concerns, I really do, but I, you nor anybody else should have to live their lives in fear.

"I am a Journalist, a profession that you were never happy about. I deliver news – not babies – Mother, and I'm not going to ignore a story because some element of danger exists.

"I had ambivalent feelings at first. I was apprehensive and fearful, but I thought about my father and his medical profession.

Daddy was good, and he was sought after all over this country because of his knowledge and skills.

"He had it made, and could have taken the easy way out. All he had to do was perform one surgical phenomenon, fly all over the country to lecture about it, and his check was written.

"Daddy chose not to do that. Instead he built and operated a clinic down in the *hood,* Mother, the 'Inner City' – where danger permeates the neighborhoods, street corners, schools, grocery stores and playgrounds.

"But how could you know that Mother? You and your bourgeois club friends never took the time to frequent those areas. Why? Because it was too *dangerous.*

"Where do you think that African Americans would be today if Harriet Tubman, Frederick Douglass, Martin Luther King Jr., Malcolm X, Marcus Garvey and others, had decided not to get involved and make their contributions to society because it was too *dangerous?*

"I love you very much, and I appreciate your concern, but this is me, Mother. This is who I am and what I do."

"Well, I guess enough has been said. I don't see where you'll change your mind. I don't even know why I thought you would," said Mrs. Lewis somberly.

Jade thought, *Okay here we go; phase one was the aggressor, phase two was the sympathizer. Now we're on phase three, and she is about to feel sorry for herself. Finally she will go to phase four and become totally obnoxious.*

Jade smiled to herself because she knew this call would end shortly.

"I love you too darling, Carol Lewis said. I will be a total wreck here all by myself, wondering if you'll be all right. Why can't you move back home, get married, have some babies and work for the Chicago Tribune."

Jade responded, "Mom, why do we go through this every time we talk? Haven't you heard anything that I said? Why can't you just respect my decisions?"

Mrs. Lewis responded with a raised voice, "Respect your decisions? Jade, you don't even know how to make decisions – not proper ones anyway! You are so much like your father; I can't tell you anything that's good for you. Just like you let Kim talk

you into cutting all that pretty long hair off for some kind of twisted up, nappy – looking hairstyle.

"You need to improve your image. You're thin as a rail, you need to eat better and get more sleep, – and what about a boyfriend? You are still young and you need to be dating. It's time for you to start thinking about getting married. Pretty soon you will be too old.

"I know you aren't listening, Jade, but I just want you to be happy. Well, I have a meeting to attend, call me this weekend with your new telephone number. Love you darling."

"Goodbye, Mother, and I love you too," Jade said, exhausted and relieved that the conversation was over. She would always feel anxiety after her mother's phone calls, and today was no exception. She felt a headache coming on, and began searching her purse for some aspirin.

It was Thursday morning, and Jade woke up to the radio's alarm clock. The Tom Joyner morning show was on. She had taken off from work for the rest of the week in preparation to move. It had been a while since she could just lie in bed, and not

have to go anywhere. It felt good, and she decided that she would lay there as long as her body would take it.

As she listened to Tom and his crew laughing, and making jokes, her mind drifted back to the telephone conversation with her mother the day before.

Maybe her mother was right she thought. She was twenty-six years old, without a boyfriend – or even a prospect for a date, and she was getting older.

The last time that she had dated someone was more than a year ago. His name was David Woods and he worked for the *Gazette* also. David moved on to a paper in Dallas to be near his family.

He had asked her to marry him and move to Texas but she wasn't in love with David. She liked him a lot, but she was not ready to get married. He still called her occasionally, and she enjoyed talking with him, but that's as far as it went.

Jade thought about Phillip, Mama Jo's son. She wondered if he had a girlfriend or if he was a player.

He was too fine not to have anybody – and being in his profession, she imagined that he met women all the time.

Mama Jo wouldn't have mentioned him being single if he had a girlfriend, I don't guess, but he's probably a player, **she thought. Just then another thought occurred to her.** ***Since Phillip was a detective, and grew up in the neighborhood, he should know Albright – and could probably give her some information that would help with the story.***

She planned to call him after she moved in. Maybe she would invite him over for a drink, so that they could discuss the situation.

She laughed to herself as she thought about how Kim had marveled over him. Kim seemed to be interested in getting to know him better – and he appeared to be interested in her.

Maybe he had a friend that he could introduce to her, and they could all get together for a drink.

Jade decided to get up, and start packing. She had already made arrangements with the moving company, and planned to take some things to her new place, later that day. But first she felt the need to call David in Texas.

"Hello, this is David Woods," the voice on the other line said.

"Hi David, this is Jade. How are you?" Jade said as she plumped up her pillows to get more comfortable in bed.

David was excited to hear her voice. "Hey Jade – what's going on, baby? Please tell me you are calling to say that you are ready to get married and move to Dallas."

Jade laughed. He could always make her laugh. "No David, that's not why I'm calling. I just feel the need to share some of my excitement with you – and to, of course, get your level – headed opinion. But first, tell me what's going on with you, how's your job going, and how's your family doing?"

David responded, "Everybody is good. I'm a new uncle, my sister had a baby girl, yesterday. My mother finally seems to be adjusting to my father's death. She doesn't depend on me as much now that we've gotten her involved with this senior citizen program. She has a social life busier than mine. The job is good; I got promoted to section editor last week."

Jade interrupted, "Congratulations, David! Why didn't you call and let me know, or e-mail me or something? I'm so proud of you – and if anybody deserves that position, it's you. I know you and your friend celebrated. She must be proud of you too."

He responded, "Thank you Jade. That's very kind of you to say. It means a lot. I had planned to call you. In fact, I was going to give you a call this weekend. You must have felt my vibes and called me instead.

"And what are you talking about, 'my friend'? How do you know I have one? You're just trying to be nosey, aren't you?"

Jade laughed again, "No I'm not trying to be nosey. I guess I was just assuming. I was hoping that one of us got lucky and found somebody special. I'll probably be single for the rest of my life."

"You must have talked with your mother recently. She's the only person that can put you in that mood where you feel sorry for yourself.

"You don't have to be single, Jade – it's your choice to be. You won't allow time for anyone – you are too busy working, and you need to relax, to start enjoying life." David said.

"When was the last time you went out on a date? When was the last time you were kissed? And when was the last time you actually got excited about going out shopping to buy a new outfit

because you had this hot date – and you wanted to look extra good?" David asked.

"Dang! You sure know how to make a girl feel bad! My mother wasn't *that* cold, and I didn't mean anything by what I said, I was merely making conversation. I won't ask you about your personal life again." Jade snapped, her feelings were slightly hurt.

David sensed her annoyance and apologized, "Jade, I'm sorry, I got carried away. Listen girl, I care for you – and I want to see you happy, whether it's with me or whoever. All I'm saying is that you need a life outside of the *Gazette.*

"Yes, I've met someone and she is special – but Jade if you just say the word, I would marry you in a New York minute – and you know that. I'm still in love with you girl."

Jade became silent. She didn't intend for the conversation to come to this point.

After a moment she spoke, "David, you are special to me – and you know that, but you and I aren't destined to be together. I don't know what's in store for me, and I'm glad that you've found that special someone. When I meet Mr. Right, David, I will

know it. I will feel it, and I will certainly call you to tell you about it."

David laughed, and wished she was in his presence. He wanted to hug her. "I know you would call me, Jade. Now tell me, what's this exciting news all about?"

Jade began to tell him about the assignment and her new apartment. In spite of her brief moment of anger with David, she wanted his opinion. She respected his judgment.

After listening to Jade, David responded, "This assignment is tailor – made for you Jade. Bob made the right choice, but don't go in with blinders on.

"This sound like it could be a little bit dangerous – so please be careful and stay focused. Don't go meddling into something that's not relevant. You don't know when to quit sometimes, Jade. You know I'm right, but I trust that you've matured, and you'll do a hell of a good job. I know you will."

Jade needed to hear that. Before she hung up the telephone, she thanked him.

CHAPTER IV

THE MOVE

It was Friday, a sunny but crisp October morning. It was a good day for moving, Jade thought, as she carried boxes from her car into her new place. The moving van had already been there to deliver her furniture and Kim, who had taken off from work earlier, helped her to get everything set up.

Kim had also secretly hoped to get a glimpse of Phillip, but she had a dental appointment and had to leave early. After Jade shared her plans with Kim to invite Phillip over for a drink, and to solicit his help with her investigation, Kim decided not to say anything about the crush she had on him.

He had been on her mind ever since she and Jade met him – but it never occurred to her that Jade might be interested in him also. She planned to discuss this issue with her friend at a later time.

But not now, Jade was too preoccupied with moving and Kim didn't want to distract her.

Jade was making the last trip to her car when she noticed Mama Jo getting out of a car with a young woman. They began taking packages, which appeared to be groceries out of the trunk.

"Need any help?" Jade called out to the two women.

Mama Jo looked over and said, "No thank you, baby. We only have a few packages. Do you need any help? Sorry nobody was here to help you out, but I had a doctor's appointment, and Jennifer stopped me by the market to pick up a few groceries."

***So that's Jennifer, Mama Jo's granddaughter,* Jade thought.**

"Come over here, Jade. I want you to meet my grandbaby," Mama Jo said, smiling. "Jennifer this is Jade, the sweet little thing, I was telling you about."

The girl put the bag of groceries that she had taken out of the trunk of the car on the hood, and extended her hand to Jade, "Hello Jade, I feel like I know you already, Mama has been going on and on about you ever since you came by to rent the apartment."

Jade took her hand and said, "Your grandmother is a sweetheart, and I feel honored. I'm just about finished, are you sure you don't need me to help you?"

"Chile, you mean you moved everything in already?" Mama Jo asked, as she walked to the porch.

"Yes ma'am, but I had some help – and remember I started bringing some things over yesterday. Kim was here earlier and she was a big help, but she had to leave, she asked me to say hello for her. You remember Kim don't you Mama Jo?" Jade asked.

"Sure I do, she's a sweet little thing, too. Mama Jo said.

"Well, we got everything in place except for my computer and computer furniture; and it should be delivered at any moment. I'm also waiting for the telephone man," Jade continued to explain.

"Why don't you come on in and have some tea while you are waiting for the people," Mama Jo asked.

"Okay, but let me take these things upstairs and lock the doors, I'll be there shortly," Jade responded.

Mama Jo and Jennifer had just about put everything away when Jade walked in. "I brought some herbal tea for you to try

out. This is what I drink every morning before my run, and I swear, it helps to get me going."

"What is the name of it?" asked Jennifer.

"Tea Mate," Jade answered. The herbs in the tea are found in the deep forest somewhere in India, and have been used for centuries; it's good for boosting energy and mental alertness."

"If it can boost energy, then pour me a gallon, where do you buy it?" Jennifer asked.

"From any health food store. I noticed there's one in the village, and I plan to go and check it out. Would you like for me to let you know when I go, and we can go together?" Jade asked.

"That would be nice. You're talking about Wild Herbs health foods. I've been in there before. Are you into health foods Jade?" Jennifer asked.

"No, not really. I buy fruit and tea mostly, but when I run across something interesting, I might pick that up. How about you – are you into herbs?" Jade asked.

Realizing she should have rephrased that question said, "I mean,"

Jennifer interrupted by laughing and said, "I know what you mean. Yes, I am into herbs – and not the kind that's in your tea. What about you, do you smoke?"

Jade, feeling a little embarrassed, but intrigued by Jennifer's answer, responded, "No, I don't smoke. I have tried it, but it makes me sleepy, and unfocused."

Mama Jo was in the kitchen heating up the tea kettle. She was so happy the girls seemed to be getting along, she could hear them laughing. She liked that because Jennifer didn't laugh much. She was a quiet girl.

The girls went into the den, where Jennifer was showing off her collection of CD's. They both loved music, and had some of the same ones.

Jade started looking at the family photo's and asked, "Do you have any brother or sisters?"

Jennifer responded, "I have an older brother. His name is Kevin. He used to live upstairs, but he moved out with his girlfriend, who looks older than—"

Jade interrupted, "I know – than Mama Jo."

The girls broke into laughter again. They really seemed to be enjoying each other.

"You mean Mama told you about that," Jennifer said.

"Well, I don't know why I'm surprised; she doesn't hide her feelings about that situation. I think Kevin leaving really hurt her. She raised us you know, and we're all that she has – and my Uncle Phillip."

At that moment, Jade felt strange. She couldn't put her finger on what it was, but it was as if someone else had walked into the room. After a moment, she shrugged it off. She wanted to ask about her parents, but decided not to, she was sure it would come up later.

"Your Uncle Phillip is *fine* girl! I bet he has a lot of girlfriends," Jade said slyly.

Jennifer, picking up the vibe, said, "I hear where you're coming from, but I'm not going there. He does his own thing around here, and I'm not one to tell."

"Sorry, I didn't mean to be nosey. It's a bad habit with me, you see, I'm a journalist, and asking questions is part of the job," Jade said.

Jennifer looked at Jade, and asked, "Are you on the job now?"

Jade paused for a moment, unsure of what to say.

Just then Mama Jo called out, "Tea Time!"

Both girls walked into the dining area, and sat at the table. Mama Jo had poured the hot water into three beautiful china tea cups. Jade placed tea bags and sweet stevia into each of their cups.

"You girls sure seemed to be having a good time. I haven't heard Jennifer laugh like that in years," Mama Jo commented.

"Jade is quite a conversationalist – and she is very inquisitive, but I enjoyed our little session," Jennifer said as she sipped her tea.

Jade sat speechless, she couldn't feel where Jennifer was coming from. One minute they were laughing, and the next, Jennifer was blasting her for getting too personal. Then she tells Mama Jo, she enjoyed their "little session."

Jade was confused about Jennifer, as she looked across the table at her. Jennifer was fair–skinned, and wore her shoulder

length hair straight. She was thin, just like Mama Jo said, but not anorexic. Her eyes were large and hazel.

Jade thought she was a beautiful girl, but she seemed complex, and strange. Yet there was something eerily familiar about Jennifer.

Mama Jo broke the silence. "This tea sure is good. I'm going to have to get me some."

Jennifer smiled and said, "Jade, don't forget to let me know when you go, so I can go with you. I just might want to pick me up an herb or two."

She looked at Jade and started laughing.

Jade, unsure of what to say, decided after a moment, to laugh along with her. Mama Jo laughed also, oblivious to what they were talking about, and oblivious to what was going on.

Kevin walked into the dining room and asked, "What's going on in here? Ya'll laughing so loud, you didn't here me come in the door."

He leaned over to kiss Mama Jo on her cheek, then walked over to his sister, and gave her a hug and kiss. He looked at Jade,

held his hand out, and said, "You must be Jade. I've heard a lot about you. I'm Kevin, Jen's brother."

"Nice to meet you, Kevin, and I've heard a lot about you too," Jade said, as she extended her hand. Jennifer and Mama Jo started to giggle.

"I know Mama and Jen's been talking about my old lady," Kevin said. "She's all right. She's a good girl – just a little bit older than I am."

"A little *bit* older Kevin? Try four years. She's almost Uncle Phillip's age," Jennifer said, as she rose up from her chair.

They all laughed. Jade noticed how extremely close this family seemed to be. She wished she had that kind of relationship with her mother.

"Mama, Jen sure is in a good mood, what's up with that?" Kevin asked.

"I'm always in a good mood, what are you talking about – and you all are giving Jade the wrong impression of me." Jennifer said, playfully hitting at Kevin.

She looked at Jade, and said, "Pay them no attention. I really am a nice person."

Mama Jo, responding to Kevin, said, "It is good to see her laughing and having a good time, and we have Jade to thank for that."

Kevin shook his head in agreement as he and Jennifer walked towards the door. Kevin worked as a mechanic. He had come by to look at his sister's car, which had been causing her some problems.

Jade smiled, as she watched the two walk out the door.

She told Mama Jo how lucky she was to have family that was so close. She briefly explained the relationship she had with her mother, and how difficult it was to feel close to her.

Mama Jo seemed preoccupied, as she poured hot water into their cups for more tea.

"Are you alright, Mama Jo?" Jade asked, as she observed her.

"I'm fine, baby – just fine. Sometimes my mind drifts away," she responded.

"I hope I didn't offend Jennifer, I don't think she liked me asking so many questions, Mama Jo. I warned her reporters tend to do that. We just can't seem to separate that part of our job from the rest of our lives," Jade explained.

Mama Jo laughed and said, "Chile, you didn't offend Jennifer. She wouldn't have sat around with us if she was offended. She would have left the table. You made her laugh and not too many people have been able to do that, not since that – that awful thing happened to her."

Mama Jo paused, closed her eyes, and tightened her lips for a second. Then she continued. "I had been worried about Jennifer, especially after Tom died. They were very close. Basically, she is a quiet girl and stays to herself, but here lately, she's been in some pretty good moods. She really felt comfortable with you today, I could tell. Poor chile, I feel so sorry for her. She's had so much to deal with in her life."

Jade wanted so bad to ask Mama Joe what she was talking about – and she also wanted to ask what had happened to Jennifer, and about her parents.

She wondered if Jennifer suffered from depression. She definitely had mood swings – Jade saw that today. She wanted to ask so many questions, but obviously, this family had experienced some deep, emotional pain.

She was too fond of Mama Jo to keep bringing up bad memories. Jade decided this family would be off-limits for questions pertaining to her story, she would find other sources.

Mama Jo's doorbell rang, it was the telephone man, from Bell South. He was looking for Jade Lewis.

Jade thanked Mama Jo for inviting her over, and left. She waved at Kevin and Jennifer as she climbed the stairs to let the telephone man in. The computer and desk arrived shortly thereafter.

Later on that night as Jade stepped out of the shower to dry off, she heard a car door shut. She threw on her pink silk bathrobe, walked over to the window, and noticed that it was Jennifer leaving in her car. *Wonder where she's going? Probably to the store,* Jade thought.

Just then, the telephone rang, Jade wondered who that could be.

"Hello," she said.

"Hey Jade, this is Kim. How's everything going? I see you have your phone service, did your computer come?"

Jade, glad to here her friend's voice responded, "Yes, it came about an hour or so after you left. I didn't get a chance to say thank you, but girl you really helped me out. How about dinner and drinks tomorrow evening – on me? You can choose the place."

"It's a date – and don't forget to bring your American Express card. What time are we talking about?" Kim asked.

"Does six o'clock sound good?" asked Jade.

"Sure does, I'll see you then," Kim replied.

"I'll pick you up at five thirty," Jade said as she hung up the phone.

Jade put in a CD and fixed a cup of tea. She looked around her apartment and she was pleased. Although she wasn't finished with all the rooms, she had completed the living room and her bedroom.

She had a beige – colored sectional – sofa, with several multi-colored pillows, in shades of mint green, rose and lilac, tossed about. Jade loved black – abstract art. She had two prints, displayed in large gold picture frames, on the wall behind the sofa.

There was a mahogany wood, wall unit, containing her sound system, television and several glass bottles, displayed on the shelves. The bottles were in the same shades of her pillows and of various shapes and sizes.

Jade had mahogany wood end tables, with two ceramic lamps on each of them. Her cordless phone unit sat on one of the tables.

Jade's bedroom was decorated in oriental motif.

"BUZZZZZZ," **the clock radio went off, Jade was startled as she rolled over to see what time it was. She didn't even remember setting her clock.**

The voice of Tom Joyner came over the radio. Jade lay there, contemplating on whether to get up or not and go for her morning run.

After a few minutes, she decided to get up. She thought this would be a good time for her to familiarize herself with the neighborhood.

Jade washed her face and threw on her sweats. It was a little chilly so she decided to layer her clothing. As she ran down the

stairs to the end of the driveway she paused, trying to decide which way she would go.

Jade thought it would be best to go down Montrose, and then take some of the side streets that would lead her to 12th Street, and then back to Montrose. She would run for about forty – five minutes.

As she proceeded down Montrose, she noticed the many different types of houses along the street. They were all – older, but very, well preserved and like Mama Jo's, the lawn's were very well manicured. There was an assortment of trees; all bearing beautiful fall – colored leaves symbolizing the changing of the season.

It was a beautiful morning to run, and as Jade trotted passed each house, she wondered which ones belonged to Lester Albright. She was so caught up in her thoughts that she didn't even notice the black BMW with the dark – tinted windows that was sitting at the four – way stop.

Just as she approached the four way intersection, the BMW started moving slowly across the street, and this caught Jade's eye.

That's a sharp looking car, **she thought.** ***Wonder why that person is driving so slowly. Maybe I can see who it is driving when they pass.***

As the BMW passed Jade, she was unable to see through the windows because of the dark tinting. She turned and watched the car go slowly up Montrose towards 12th Street. Jade stood for a moment before crossing the street. She wondered if the car would turn around and come back, but it didn't.

She continued her run, and as she crossed 11th and Montrose, Jade noticed a house being renovated on the corner. She wondered if Albright's company was involved with this venture.

There were several guys standing in the front yard. As she came upon the house, someone in the group whistled.

As Jade was about to pass, a man stepped out and said, "Whoa, – slow down, Ms. Lady – and let me introduce myself."

Jade was use to men flirting with her, and under normal circumstances, she would have played it off and kept going. However, this was different. She was curious, and felt the need to stop.

As the man walked to her, she noticed that he wasn't dressed like the other men. He had on an expensive blue denim outfit that was heavily starched, with the name *Sean John*, stitched in white thread on one side of his jacket.

Underneath he wore a white sweater, and had a large platinum chain with a huge diamond cross around his neck. The closer he got to her; she could see the large diamond earring on one of his earlobes.

He was very neatly dressed – and wasn't a bad looking guy, but he definitely wasn't her type, she thought.

He extended his hand out to Jade and said, "Hello, my name is Fresh – and may I have the pleasure of knowing your name?"

Jade laughed, as she thought, *No gold teeth? This man actually has no gold or platinum teeth!*

"What you smiling about, "pretty lady?" Fresh asked.

Jade quickly responded, "Oh nothing, you just reminded me of someone, that's all." She took his hand. "Hi, I'm Jade Lewis."

"Who do I remind you of, Jade Lewis? One of your old boyfriends?" he asked.

Jade thought, *Not hardly!* Then trying to change the subject, she asked, "Is this your place?"

Fresh, licking his lips, and staring at Jade's mouth, responded "One of them. You're new around here, aren't you? I saw you moving in yesterday. You could have moved in one of my places – free of charge."

"How many places do you have?" Jade asked, trying to get as much information out of him as she could – because she did not want to have too many more conversations with Fresh.

"Quite a few," he answered. We have several on some of the other streets in this neighborhood, and several here on Montrose."

"We, who? I thought you said these were *your* places. Are you working with someone else?" Jade asked curiously.

Fresh was caught off guard; the question came faster than he could think. He was becoming flustered, but he wanted to remain cool in front of her.

"Yeah, I got a partner," he replied. "He handles the business end of it, and I handle the construction end."

Just then, one of the men called for Fresh. "Look, I gotta go, why don't you give me that number, and we can continue this conversation over dinner."

Jade did not care to give him her telephone number so she used one of her old lines, and said, "Sorry Fresh, but my phone is not connected yet, see you around."

Before he could respond, she began jogging down the street. Although Jade was relieved Fresh had to go, she wished she had gotten more information.

She wondered if he and his partner were the ones who had bought Albright's business. But she had time to find out; she knew she would run into Fresh again.

In the meantime, Jade would call Scooter, her photographer, and have him to take pictures of this house.

As Jade ran past several more houses, she saw it – the house Lester Albright built. She knew it was the one, because it stuck out like a sore thumb.

It wasn't fancy at all. It was just a brand – new house sitting oddly among the older homes. She made a mental note, to have Scooter – take a picture of this house as well.

The house sat back up in the yard, and trees and shrubbery were planted all over the front lawn. There was a concrete driveway curving around to the side of the house. It widened in front of a two – car garage.

Jade slowed down as she stared at the house. *Wonder who lives here,* she thought. It didn't appear anyone was at home.

As she stood there, she tried to visualize the elderly couple's modest little home that once stood in this place. A home that had been built with hard earned money, only to be taken away so easily by deceptive practices – and now replaced by this imposing distraction.

Jade noticed the initials L.A. on the mailbox and wondered if they belonged to the current owners – or were they the initials of Lester Albright?

She tried to envision the murder scene. The car sitting in front of his house, holding his dead body.

***Was he shot in the car, or somewhere else and then placed there,* she pondered. She needed a copy of the police report, and she would research this information on the Net.**

"Can I help you with something," a frail voice asked.

Jade was startled, and turned to see who it was. A small – framed elderly black man was standing in the yard with a rake in his hand. He had appeared out of nowhere.

"Oh no sir, I was just admiring your house, and as I was jogging by, I noticed how different it was from the other houses, that's what made me stop." Jade said nervously.

The elderly man snapped, "Dis' ain't my house, I just take care of the land. Dis' here is a *evil house,* and if I was you, I wouldn't stand round here too long."

Jade was surprised to hear him say that – and asked with a bit of sarcasm, "What do you mean, it's an evil house? Are there ghosts here that will come out and get me if I don't leave? And since this is not your house, then who does it belong to?"

The man stared at Jade for a moment, and then became irritated and said, "Miss, I done told you dis' was a *evil house.* Dat's all you need to know – and if I was you, I wouldn't concern myself bout' who lives here."

Then he turned and walked away. Jade called out to him several times, but he ignored her, and kept walking until he was out of sight.

Thinking about what the old man had just said, reality set in, and Jade became frightened. She felt eeriness around her, and decided to take his advice and leave.

As she continued her run, all she could think about was what the little old man had said – and she wondered what exactly he meant about the house being evil.

CHAPTER V

THE BLACK BMW

Jade and Kim were sipping on Chardonnay when the waiter took their orders for lobster tails and crab legs. Kim had chosen her favorite restaurant, the Fisherman's Wharf.

Jade, as usual, had filled Kim in on what had happened since she last spoke with her. Kim felt uneasy about the black BMW slowly driving by Jade, and about the old man who was working in the yard of the house that Albright once owned.

She was trying to convince her to tell Sean and Bob about it. "Jade, listen to me, honey. Your safety matters most to me in this situation. I think you should call Sean and Bob, first thing Monday morning, and let them know about this car. At least let them check out the license plate number.

"I know someone at the motor vehicle place. They can put in the license number and get all kinds of information on this

person. Will you at least let me do that for you?" Kim asked, obviously concerned.

Jade responded, "It can be frightening, but nothing happened. They didn't stop or try to do anything to me. I feel like it might be something else – but I can't put my finger on it.

"Anyway, what bothers me the most is what the little old man said about the house, now *that* is scary. However, just to ease your mind, Kim, I will try to get the license number. I could get this information myself, but since you want to help me out, you can check it out for me with your sources.

"I will talk to Sean and Bob about both incidents, but I just don't want any unnecessary worrying. My intuition tells me that it's really nothing to worry about."

Kim felt relieved and commented, "You and your intuition. I have to admit girl, most of the time you are right on cue, except when—."

"Except when what," Jade interrupted. "What are you talking about, I'm always in tune with my spirit, girlfriend – *my higher power.*"

Jade smiled, and took a sip from her glass. Kim tried to contain her laughter and said in a very sassy tone, "Was it your intuition, your spirit and your higher power that led you to meet your new boyfriend, Fresh?"

They both laughed and Jade, feeling very relaxed responded, "Girl, you mean my boy who was dressed clean in his denim jeans, iced and platinum down, bling-blinging and didn't have a grill in his mouth?"

Kim was starting to feel the effects of her drink also, "Girl, I can't believe he didn't have a gold or platinum grill. I just knew when he opened his mouth, you would be able to see your reflection! Jade, I knew you were desperate for a man, but – *Fresh?"*

Jade shot back, "Well Kim, I guess I was just *Fresh* out of choices."

They were laughing so hard that neither of them noticed the waiter standing at their table with their food, and a bottle of Kendall Jackson Chardonnay. The wine was sent to their table by a very handsome man, who was sitting at the bar.

"Excuse me ladies, the gentleman at the bar sent this to you. Will you accept?" the waiter asked, smiling.

"Of course we accept!" Kim said, as she took the chardonnay, from the waiter. Who did you say sent it?"

Before the waiter could respond, the man walked up to their table, and spoke in a deep, seductive voice. "Good evening, I hope I'm not imposing on you two beautiful ladies by sending this wine over, but I couldn't help but notice that you both seem to really be enjoying yourselves. I like to see people having a good time."

As they both thanked him, he grabbed Jade's hand and kissed it, looking deep into her eyes, he said, "The pleasure is mine, and you ladies have a nice rest of the evening, I'll see you around," he winked his eye at Jade, then turned and walked away.

Jade and Kim sat there in awe as they watched this mysterious man leave the restaurant.

"Who was that?" Kim looked at Jade and asked.

"I don't know," answered Jade, who was sniffing the hand that he had kissed. "But he sure smelled good."

Kim couldn't believe what she was hearing. "Jade are you crazy? You gonna' let a light, bright, damn – near white, curly –

head, good smelling, Armani suit wearing, drop dead *fine brother* who ordered you a bottle of wine, and kissed your hand, just walk out of this place? And all you can say is *'he sure smelled good.'*"

Jade, looking perplexed shrugged and asked, "What am I suppose to do, run out the door after him?"

"Why not? Girl – make your move! Go get his name, or get something! I would have beaten him to the door – and opened it up for him!" Kim responded, throwing her hands up in the air.

Jade smiled at her friend and said, "Kim think about it, that brother is trying to play us. If he wanted to know my name, he would have asked. If he wanted me to have his name, he would have introduced himself.

He intended to do exactly what he did. You heard him when he said, 'I'll see you around.' That means he'll find me again – and I'll just wait until then. He's fine and all, but he's got more play in him than a two – year – old, and I don't need that kind of drama."

"I feel you, girlfriend, Kim said. "You are too cool. I guess I was just too caught up with how the brother looked, rather than seeing just what the brother was looking like."

"Kim, I read people all the time, it's part of my training, you have to be in tune with your senses, and study people or – they will take advantage of you." Jade responded.

"I know that's right," Kim said.

As she was listening to Jade, she thought this would be a good time to bring up Phillip. "Jade, I've been meaning to ask you about Phillip, are you still planning to ask him over for drinks?"

Jade laughed, and said, "No, Kim, I'm not interested in Phillip. That's what you really want to ask – and I told you, Mama Jo and her family are off limits. They've been through enough – and that includes Phillip, too, so go ahead as you say – '*Make your move.*"

Kim smiled, and playfully said, in her ghetto voice, "You better be glad dat' you ain't got your eyes on my man, girlfriend, cause I was about to git' all up in yo' business."

Jade looked at Kim and said, "Ooh, I'm scared of you." They both laughed.

When they finished their dinner and drinks, Jade and Kim, headed home. They had enjoyed themselves immensely.

After Jade had dropped Kim off, she was driving on 12th Street towards home when she noticed through her rearview mirror that the black BMW was behind her.

She wasn't sure if it was following her, or just happened to be behind her. She noticed that it would drive up close to her rear end, and then back off.

This happened several times. She became frightened, and decided to drive a little faster. Her heart was pounding; perspiration filled the palm of her hands as she gripped the steering wheel.

Jade finally reached Montrose, and turned left onto the street. She felt safe then, so she slowed down and looked behind her.

The car was gone. She wasn't sure which way it went and she didn't care either, as long as it wasn't behind her. Jade pulled into the driveway, and before she got out of her car, she looked all around her to make sure she was safe.

When she didn't see anyone, Jade jumped out of her car, ran up the stairs – into her apartment, and immediately locked the doors.

It was Sunday morning, and Mama Jo had left a message Saturday night for Jade on her voice mail, to call her. Jade was too tired to talk when she got in last night, and planned to call her in the morning.

***I'll just stop by Mama Jo's before I go jogging to see what she wants,* thought Jade.**

She laid in bed for a few more minutes, she was still feeling the effects of the Chardonnay from last night. Jade really didn't feel like jogging, but she made herself get up, and she drank several cups of tea before she ran.

As she started down her stairs, she saw Mama Jo on the front porch.

"Good morning Mama Jo, I was just on my way down to your house, I got your message – but it was late when I got in," Jade said.

Mama Jo was dressed for church and had her Bible in tow. She was calling for Jennifer to hurry up so she wouldn't be late for Sunday school.

"Good morning to you, baby. I called you last night, to invite you to church this morning – or any morning you feel like going," Mama Jo said to Jade.

"Jennifer, you come on now, I don't want to miss my class," Mama Jo cried out.

"That's so sweet of you to invite me to your church, how about next Sunday, I'll go with you then. You look mighty pretty in your gold suit and hat. You better watch out for those deacons, they are going to be all over you, Mama Jo," Jade said teasingly.

"Bless your heart chile, but honey, those deacons are too old for Mama Jo – and I don't want nothing old but money," Mama Jo said as she giggled.

Jade laughed along with her, and said, "I hear you, Mama Jo, I hear you."

"I don't mean to worry you either, about church," Mama Jo said. "But I do want you to go, so whenever you ready, just let me know.

"Why don't you come to dinner today at three? You need to eat right. You and Jennifer both running around here looking like

little birds. I've cooked a big Sunday dinner, and I want you to come and eat with us," Mama Jo said.

Jade hugged and kissed Mama Jo on her cheek and accepted her invitation to dinner. She asked if she should bring something and Mama Jo told her no. Jade then began her morning jog, and as she trotted off, Mama Jo watched her and smiled. She was happy that Jade had come into their lives.

Jade felt very blessed this morning. She had moved into a place that she absolutely adored, and she had met people who accepted her like family. Everything seemed to be falling in place. Now all she had to do was concentrate on her story.

As Jade crossed 11th and Montrose, she looked at the empty house being renovated on the corner. Without the construction crew working, it looked so desolate.

She wondered who lived there prior to the renovations. *Did they own it and perhaps lost it to one of Albright's home renovation scams? Were Fresh and his partner the people who took over Albright's business?*

These questions floated around in her head, and she planned to find out the answers when she ran into Fresh again. As Jade

approached the house that Albright built, she could see a dark car parked in the driveway in front of the garage.

Good, somebody is home. Maybe I will get a chance to see the people who live there, **she thought. However, the closer Jade came to the house, the clearer the image of the car became.**

It was the black BMW that had been following her.

Fear gripped Jade's body, but she didn't panic. Jade thought that at any moment the person driving that car would come out of the door, so she closed her eyes and took several deep breaths.

All of a sudden, the fear dissipated, and when Jade opened her eyes, she looked at the car, then at the house. She didn't see anyone, and she began to move. Jade didn't run very fast, but she jogged steadily until she reached Montrose and her apartment.

As Jade climbed the stairs to her apartment, she felt drained. Instead of going inside, she sat down at the top of the stairs. She needed to think, to put things in perspective.

"Was it a coincidence that the same person following her in the black car happened to live in Albright's old house? Who was it and why would they want to follow her in the first place? What was the connection – and what did all of this mean?"

Jade was convinced this person didn't know about her, or the story. She had not talked with anyone in the neighborhood about it. She was confused, and she couldn't make sense of any of it.

As Jade sat on the stairs, she decided she would not allow this person in the black car to intimidate her any longer.

Jade went inside of her apartment, and got a bottle of water from the refrigerator. She sat down at the computer, and typed in a few notes, before she picked up the telephone and dialed Scooter's number.

Scooter is a 30 – something year old photographer for the Nashville *Gazette.* He has been there for twelve years, and is highly respected for his work. He is known as one of the best photographers in the industry.

Scooter, whose real name is, Jeffrey Marco, is a tall, lanky Jamaican, with a no – nonsense attitude. He acquired his nickname from his colleagues, because of the way he shuffled his feet.

After six rings, Jade was about to hang up the phone, when suddenly, a voice with a thick Jamaican accent picked up. "Speak to me."

Jade, unfamiliar with Scooter's voice, hesitated before responding. "Hello, my name is Jade Lewis, whom am I speaking with?"

"Wit whom, do you wish to speak wit mon?" the person asked.

"I'm trying to reach Jeffrey Marco, is he in?" Jade asked, intrigued by this distinguished sounding voice.

"I am. Hello, Ms. Jade. I've been awaiting yuh call, ahn please call me Scooter," he responded.

"Okay Scoo-tah," Jade answered jovially, imitating his accent.

She and Scooter spent the next thirty minutes on the phone, collaborating on how best to illustrate the series. Afterwards, Jade took a shower and napped before going to dinner at Mama Jo's.

Jade decided to wear a pair of black dress slacks, a black and white zebra print sweater, and black leather boots. She had washed her hair, which had grown quite a bit since she last had it professionally done, so she decided to wear it down, and naturally wavy.

As Jade was leaving her apartment, she noticed Phillip and another man getting out of his car.

"Hey, Jennifer," Phillip said waving.

Jade smiled and said, "Phillip, this is Jade."

As the two men got closer to her, Phillip realized he had called her the wrong name, he put his arm around her shoulder, and said, "Jade I apologize. You looked like Jennifer from a distance coming down those stairs. You've changed your hairstyle, haven't you? That's what threw me off; you had it all curly and twisted the last time I saw you."

Jade, feeling a little paranoid about her hair, responded, "This is what happens to you when you neglect your hair appointments."

"I think you have a gorgeous head of hair, I like the way it looks," said the other man.

Phillip, realizing he had not introduced them, quickly responded, "Man I'm sorry. This is Jade Lewis, the young lady I was telling you about who just moved in. Jade, this is Brian Williams, a friend and colleague."

They shook hands and exchanged greetings. Jade thought Brian was a very handsome man, even more so than Phillip.

***Now this is a chocolate dream – this brother is F-I-N-E,* she thought. She was amused by the fact she had met more good – looking men within the past week than she had in all of her twenty six years.**

***Maybe God is answering my Mother's prayers, since she is so eager for me to get married. He's sending these fine brothers for me to choose from,* she thought, as she chuckled to herself.**

The three of them went inside and greeted Mama Jo, Kevin, and Jennifer. The house was filled with the aroma of food and Jade hadn't realized just how hungry she was.

Mama Jo stood in the doorway of the kitchen, smiling. She was happy – she loved having company, and she loved cooking. Jade went into the kitchen to help Jennifer bring out the food, to put on the table.

"Look at all this food! Did Mama Jo do this by herself?" Jade asked Jennifer.

"Yeah, she always cooks like this. She loves it, and she doesn't like anybody helping her either. She'll start on Saturday, and finish up on Sunday morning," answered Jennifer.

Mama Jo had prepared fried chicken, turnip greens, macaroni and cheese, sweet potatoes, hot water corn bread, and she had baked a chess pie. The girls set the table, Phillip blessed the food and everyone began to eat.

Jade sat across from Brian, who had been watching her all afternoon – and she had been watching him also.

She thought he was sexy looking. He was about six and a half feet tall, with an athletic build, and had beautiful pearly white teeth, with perfect shaped lips.

Jade immediately thought about India Arie's song, 'Brown Skin.' Brian had a smooth, chocolate brown skin tone, and deep, dark brown, penetrating eyes. Watching him made her nervous, and as hungry as she was, she found it difficult to eat the way she would under normal circumstances. She had butterflies in her stomach.

"Phillip, I thought you were bringing your friend by for dinner. What's her name – ah, ah – Ana. What happened to her?" asked Jennifer.

Phillip smiled at Jade, and said, "I was hoping that Jade would have invited her friend Kim, since she was flirting with me so, when I first met her. I would like to get to know her better. Besides, Jennifer, you know that Ana is just a friend, nobody special."

Jade was puzzled why Jennifer would bring up that lady's name.

What was her point, maybe she was high, and didn't realize what she was saying. Perhaps, she was trying to feel me out – to see how I would react. I don't know. The girl is weird! **Jade thought.**

Jade was surprised to hear that Philip was expecting Kim to come to dinner. She wished she had called and told her, but she didn't know.

She thought that getting them together would not be difficult at all; she couldn't wait to call and tell Kim.

Jade responded to Phillip, "I would have invited her if I had known."

Mama Jo interrupted, "Forgive me baby, I should have said something to you about inviting Kim. I like her, and she's welcome here anytime – and you feel free to invite her. Maybe you, Brian Phillip, and Kim can go out together on a date sometimes.

"Lord knows they need to stop working so hard, learn to relax, and enjoy themselves with some pretty women." Everyone laughed.

Jennifer spoke up and said, "Mama, you can't be doing that, Jade and Brian might be seeing other people and they may not like each other well enough to go out on a date."

Mama Jo, still laughing, said, "They might be seeing other people, I don't know, but I do know one thing, they've been sitting here all evening eyeing and smiling at each other. That ought to tell you something honey, these eyes ain't blind yet."

"Jennifer, you know Mama don't miss nothing." Kevin said.

Jade was glad that Mama Jo had opened the door. She was hoping that Brian would be interested in her.

Just then Brian spoke up, and said, "Thank you Mama Jo, I've been sitting here trying to come up with something to say to this young lady to let her know that I was definitely interested."

Jade was speechless, but excited about what she had just heard from Brian. All she could do was smile at him.

After dinner, Jade helped Mama Jo and Jennifer clean up. She had called Kim for Phillip, and they were on the telephone talking.

Brian helped Jade wash and dry the dishes. Mama Jo was beside herself as she watched them together. Jennifer had to usher her out of the kitchen, and make her sit down to rest while she retreated to her room.

Jade, Brian and Phillip talked for what seemed like hours and Kevin had left to go home. Afterwards, Brian walked Jade outside, to her apartment.

It was late evening and the sun had gone down, leaving a slight chill in the air on this October night. The wind was blowing, and there was a full moon glaring in the distant sky.

This was a perfect moment, **Jade thought. She began reflecting on what her friend, David had asked her during their telephone conversation – about when was the last time she had been kissed.**

She was secretly hoping that it would be tonight.

As they climbed the stairs, and reached the front door to Jade's apartment, Brian asked, "Can I have your telephone number, I'd like to see you again."

"Sure. You have a pen and paper?" Jade asked.

Brian pulled a pen and piece of paper from inside his jacket. He wrote down the numbers, as Jade called them out. He gave her a hug, and kissed her on the cheek, before telling her goodnight.

As she turned her head slightly, she caught a glimpse of the black BMW slowly going up Montrose. But Jade was so caught up in the moment, seeing that car really didn't matter anymore.

She didn't know if it was because she felt safe with Brian, or if she had subconsciously made up in her mind not to be intimidated by the car's presence.

Whatever it was, Jade had decided that this moment was too important to be interrupted!

CHAPTER VI

MAKING IT HAPPEN…

The next morning, Jade had no problem getting up out of bed. She was feeling good. The morning news programs were on the television, and she had decided to make a few calls before her morning run.

Jade dialed Kim's number, she wanted to tell her about Brian.

"Hey Kim, what's going on?" Jade asked.

"No, you tell me what's going on. Is the brother fine or what? Give it up, girlfriend, I want to hear everything!" Kim said, anxiously.

Jade began to tell Kim about the dinner at Mama Jo's, and all about Brian. They talked for fifteen minutes, before another call came in.

"When Brian put his arms around me, it felt like my feet left the ground, Jade said.

They both laughed then another call beeped in. It was Brian.

"I've got to go, Brian is on the other line. I hope you and Phillip enjoy your lunch today, call me later." Jade said to Kim, and then she clicked over to the other line.

She and Brian spoke for another thirty minutes, and he had asked her out to dinner on Friday. Jade noticed that time was getting behind her and she still needed to call her mother and Sean.

"I'll be ready at seven, and I promise to tell you all about my job then, okay?" Jade said to Brian before hanging up.

Her mother was not at home, much to Jade's relief. She left her new number on her mother's voice mail.

She called Sean, who had a million questions for her. Jade decided not to tell him about the black car, or about what the old man had said about the house. She was ready to get started with this assignment, and needed as little distraction as possible.

Jade was ready to make things happen.

Before she left the house to run, Jade sat on the sofa for a few minutes, and daydreamed about Brian. She had never felt like

this before about anybody. She liked him a lot, and was not going to let him get away!

It was ten o'clock in the morning. Although it was later than she would normally run, she decided to go anyway. She was hoping to see Fresh, and try to get some more information from him.

She thought she probably missed the black car since it was so late in the morning, and she wanted to get the license number – but she knew there would be another day for that.

As Jade approached the corner of 11th and Montrose, the construction crew was already in place. Her eyes scanned the men standing in the yard until she saw Fresh, who was dressed fly as usual.

She would try to play coy with him to get his attention – she didn't want to appear too obvious. As she crossed the street, she slowed her pace. The men spotted her, and started whistling – which caught Fresh's attention.

When Jade saw him staring at her, she smiled and waved, saying, "Hey Fresh."

That was all she needed to do. He called out to her, "Good morning Ms. Jade! You looking mighty good today."

Jade stopped, and he walked up to her, and asked, "Did you get all settled in? You get that phone hooked up yet?"

Jade, trying to be as cordial as possible, said, "You look nice too Fresh, what are you up to this morning?"

Fresh, obviously taking her comment out of context responded, "Oh, not much, I just had to stop by here to check on a few things. I won't be long, and we can get together as soon as I'm finished here."

Jade played off his comment, and pretended to be interested in what he was doing.

She asked, "Are the renovations going okay? Is there a problem?"

"No Baby, everything is cool. I just needed to make sure they are staying within the budget. Sit tight a second, and let me go over these prices with my foreman – and don't you go nowhere," Fresh said as he pointed at Jade.

Jade decided to set the stage. She leaned against a parked car in front of the construction site, and positioned herself as if she

was ready to engage into a serious conversation. She crossed her arms and legs at the ankles.

When Fresh came back, he leaned on a car parked behind the one Jade was leaning on, and they began to talk. Jade was ready – and began with a barrage of questions.

"So Fresh, help me to understand some things about your business, you say you are in partnership with somebody else, right? Is it just one person or several? What kind of business is it, and what is the name of the company?"

Fresh threw his hands up in the air, and asked, "Why you asking so many questions Ms. Lady. Are you the police?"

Jade realized to get the answers, she would have to slow down, flirt a little, and throw on the charm.

She looked him square in the eye, smiled, and asked, "Fresh sweetheart, do I look like the police to you? I just find you and your work very interesting. You know not many brothers are street – smart, good looking, own a business, and are very successful, without having some kind of education."

"Whoa – now hold up my sistah, what makes you think I don't have any education. Just cause I dress like a thug, or look

like one, don't mean I am one. Let me shoot it to you straight. Naw, I don't have a BS, BA, or MBA degree – but I do have two years at NSU in accounting and finance. That's where I met Lee, my partner," Fresh said defensively.

Jade felt bad, and apologized for having making that assumption. She rubbed his arm, and asked him to forgive her.

Fresh couldn't help but to succumb to the weakness he felt for this girl. Jade knew this, and she could use it to her advantage. Now that she had his partner's first name, she could push for more information.

"My bad Fresh – I'm not knocking your hustle," she said. "You know I didn't mean anything negative. I was just complimenting you. I admire what you and Lee are doing. Did you and him drop out of school so you all could go into business together?"

Fresh, obviously trying to ignore the question asked Jade, "Did you know you had the most beautiful eyes in the world? Where you from pretty lady?"

Jade becoming a little flustered herself, realized Fresh was no fool. He was hiding something. He was not giving up information

so easily, and she would have to 'make a move,' as Kim would put it.

"I'm from Chicago," she responded. "Look Fresh, I'm just trying to keep it real, here baby. I don't usually stop and talk with every man who hollers at me. When I choose to, I would like to know everything that I can about the man – just as I expect him to want to know about me.

"The only way to find out is to ask – am I right? And if you don't have nothing to hide, then you'll have no problem answering. That's why I'm living here in Nashville now. I got involved in some mess with people *I thought I knew* in Chicago – and believe me Fresh, I'm not looking for that kind of drama anymore. Now if you'll excuse me, I'm outta here – and sorry if I wasted your time."

"Hold up Ms. Lady! I didn't mean to piss you off; I was going to answer your questions. You know you gotta be careful these days – you don't know who's who. You are a feisty little thing. I like that," Fresh said, grabbing onto Jade's arm.

Jade smiled to herself, and thought, *Whew – it worked. That was an academy-award winning performance if I have to say so*

myself. Now all I have to do is keep this façade up for a little while longer.

Fresh continued, "The name of our company is LA & Associates Mortgage Company. We make loans to people for home repairs, and we also buy houses, fix them up and resell them. Lee handles the loans and contracts, I only deal with the construction. I first met Lee at NSU. He used to be one of my clients."

Fresh started laughing at the puzzled look on Jade's face when he made that statement, and she asked, "What do you mean by, 'he used to be one of your clients?"

Fresh responded, "I didn't make enough money on my job to support myself, and pay tuition too. So I started dealing a little bit on the side. You know what I'm saying. I was selling weed to the students, who couldn't survive without a daily joint.

"After a while the demand increased, and so did my supply. I was making so much money, I was able to quit my job – and my clientele kept growing.

"Lee had been a regular, and even after he graduated, we stayed in contact and then he disappeared for about a year. One

day he caught up with me on campus, and asked if I wanted to go into business with him.

"He ran it down to me, and it sounded good. I told him I was down, you know. It's been profitable."

Jade pushed further, and went straight to the point. "Are you all scamming people – or beating them out of their property?"

"Nope." Fresh responded quickly.

"Then why are you acting so shady? I think you're hiding something. You sure you're telling me everything?" Jade asked.

Fresh was annoyed, but he still wanted to impress her. "Well, yeah, what else can I say? I mean, my Boy needed the financing – and that's all I did. He's the one who set up the business the way he wanted to run it.

"Look, I'm not up with how he handles his business, and all of that. But people sign for those loans, and if they lose their houses in the process, oh well. Don't get me wrong, I really do feel sorry for them – but hey, it's business, and that's how he chooses to handle it.

"All I did was hook him up, using my money to help him get started – and Baby, I've been paid back double. I'm still

collecting the Benjamin's – you know what I'm saying, so that's all I'm concerned with. See, Jade, in this world, nobody gives you nothing. You just gotta make things happen for ya."

Jade smiled, and thought, *How well do I know Fresh. How well do I know.*

Then she planned her exit strategy. "How many girlfriends do you have Fresh? I bet you got one on every street," Jade asked, not caring what his response would be.

Fresh was caught off guard by this question, but he came back with a quick line, "Baby I'm a single man, I run alone but I've been looking for a nice lady to call my own – and you look like you want to be spoiled. Are you down with that?"

Jade rose up from the car, took her hand and ran it under Fresh's chin, and said enticingly, "Give me your number, I'll call you."

Fresh wanted her number as well, but he didn't ask for it. He knew Jade was working him – but he didn't mind at all, he wanted this girl, and was willing to do whatever it took to get her.

As Jade turned to leave, she looked back at Fresh, and asked, "By the way Fresh. Did you know Lester Albright?"

He shrugged and answered, "I don't think so."

As Jade jogged down the street, she was trying to collect her thoughts. She was sure it was Albright's business that Fresh had bought into, but she wasn't sure how much he knew about it.

She wondered who Lee was, and where did he fit in. She was approaching the Albright house, when all of a sudden the black BMW turned quickly off Montrose, and into the driveway.

It didn't pull all the way up, and blocked the sidewalk.

Jade was startled at first, but decided to not let it bother her. The car had blocked the sidewalk, and she was unable to cross to the other side, unless she walked behind it.

She wasn't sure she wanted to do that, but as she thought about it, it would have given her an opportunity to see the license number.

Just as she was about to jog around to the back of the car, the window slowly rolled down. Jade froze in her footsteps, and anxiety filled her. All she could do was stare apprehensively inside the car.

She wondered who she was about to face, and what was planned for her. Just then, the sound of a deep male voice

penetrated her ears. She couldn't make out the words, but the voice was very familiar.

She began to focus in on the face that was staring back at her. As she looked closer at the person inside the car, she was surprised to see it was the handsome man who was at the restaurant the other night.

Jade breathed a sigh of relief, and then she exploded, "Why have you been following me? Scaring people half to death – what is wrong with you? Are you some kind of a stalker or a pervert?"

The man got out of his car apologizing. He came around to the side where Jade was standing, and said laughingly, "I am so sorry, I didn't mean to scare you. I thought you would be impressed with having a Brother driving a nice car following you around mysteriously like I've been doing."

With her hands on her hips, Jade shot back, "Impressed? You have got to be kidding me! Just who in the hell do you think you are? How was I supposed to know who you were – or *what* you were for that matter? And if you think because you are driving a BMW, somehow I'm supposed to be excited – well let me tell you

something, *Brother,* you are dead wrong. Where I'm from, you see BMW's on every corner. They come a dime a dozen."

"Man! You don't have a problem with saying what's on your mind, do you?" he replied. "If I had known that you would be this angry and upset – or that I was actually scaring you – believe me, I would have never done this to you. But I had no idea. I would have introduced myself the first day I spotted you jogging, or when I saw you at Fisherman's Wharf. Actually, I thought you were going to ask me for my name at the restaurant." the man said.

Jade was fuming, and couldn't believe this man could be so arrogant and full of himself.

"Well you thought wrong," she responded curtly. "I peeped your card, sweetheart. I knew exactly what you were doing – and trust me, I wasn't the least bit amused or impressed by you."

Jade knew she had a right to be angry, but it was more than that, she was now getting bad vibes from this man. He laughed, and attempted to place his hands on Jade's shoulders.

When she pulled back, he raised his hands and said, "Okay, okay, let's call a truce – and start all over," then he extended his hand out to Jade. "Hello my name is Lee Anderson."

Jade was about to walk away when she realized who he was. She looked over at the mailbox bearing the initials LA. She noticed them other day, and wondered what name they stood for.

***He could be the same Lee that Fresh spoke about as his business partner,* she thought. Jade's intuition kicked in. Something told her to make a quick attitude adjustment, and to stick around. She could be on to something here.**

Jade forced a smile, extended her hand, and said, "I'm Jade Lewis."

Lee lifted her hand and gently kissed it, "*Jade,* what an exotic name. It's a pleasure to finally meet you."

Jade had the feeling of deja'vu,' Lee had kissed the same hand at the restaurant the other night, and spoke with the same deep, seductive tone.

***This must be his trademark,* she thought, and she was not impressed. She would have rather taken the same hand and**

slapped him with it – but she needed him for information, so she would go along pretending.

"Please excuse my behavior, I've never experienced anything like this before, and it just frightened me," she said.

"What can I do to make it up to you? How about dinner?" he asked. It was the last thing Jade wanted to do with him, and she had to think of something quick.

"You don't owe me anything," she said. "I guess I should be impressed with all that you went through just to get my attention. How about us just being friends? I'm new in the neighborhood, and I haven't met many people around here."

Lee looked at Jade with surprise, and asked, "You've met somebody. Who was that you were hugged up with on your porch last night?"

Jade ignored his question and instead asked, "Is this your house? It is very nice – did you have it built?"

Lee appeared uncomfortable with Jade's questions and quickly answered, "No."

Jade, noticing his hesitation pushed further, "No, this is not your house, or no, you didn't build it – which one is it?"

Lee hesitated again before responding, "No, I didn't build this house. Someone else did, and yes, it belongs to me. I live here all by myself. Would you like to see it?"

Jade, as eager as she was to go inside, decided not too. She had been out long enough, and wanted to complete her run. She also thought about what the old man said about the house being evil. She wasn't sure just what she would find in there. Jade also wanted to hurry home to record notes on her computer about today's events.

"Why don't we make it another time," she asked. "I need to go home and take care of some errands."

Lee was determined to see her again, so he invited her over for drinks later that night. He was very persistent, so she agreed to come back at eight.

When Jade got home, she checked her voice mail. There were three messages from Kim, one from her mother, and one from Bob.

She decided to call Bob first.

"Robert Winslow, please. This is Jade Lewis," she said to Bob's assistant.

Almost immediately Bob was on the phone, "Jade – how's it going?"

"Everything is going better than I expected," she responded. "I seem to be literally running into the right people, and I've obtained some information that could possibly lead me to the people operating Albright's old business.

"I'm about to sort through my notes and get organized. I've got to make an appointment with someone who knew Albright. She grew up in this neighborhood, but her hair salon is closed today, so I'll give her a call on tomorrow.

"I plan to ask her about Nikki – to see if she knows anything."

Bob was impressed, "Sounds good, young lady. You move very fast. I like that. Well, I guess I'll see you on Friday, and remember Jade, whatever you need, you've got it."

Jade smiled and said, "Thank you, Bob. See you on Friday."

She decided to call her mother before calling Kim. By her leaving three messages, Kim probably had a lot to talk about.

Jade called her mother and as usual, their conversation was not pleasant. After about fifteen minutes, Jade faked a headache, and promised to call her later.

Then she called Kim at work, "Hey girlfriend, how was your lunch date?"

Kim sounding irritated, asked, "Girl – where have you been? I have called you three times."

Jade interrupted, "Whoa. Slow down! What's going on, what's the urgency?"

Kim sighed heavily and said, "I checked around to see if anybody knew Fresh – and guess what, the boy is bad news. He's a big – time drug dealer. Jade, you have got to be careful."

Jade laughed, and proceeded to thank her friend for looking out for her. "Kim, I appreciate you checking him out for me, but I think he's harmless. I actually had a very informative conversation with him today."

She proceeded to tell her about their long discussion, and how much information she was able to obtain from him including, his selling drugs when he was in college.

"He told me he used to sell drugs when was in college. He started because he wasn't making enough money working at his job, but now I don't think he's still doing it. He apparently made

a lot of money and used it to go into business with Lee. Now I think that was smart of him.

"Kim, I know we laughed at Fresh, but the boy has two years of college in finance, and he really seem to have good business sense. I think he's changed. Anyway, I'm not going to date him – all I need from him is information."

She went on to tell her about Lee also, and that she would be meeting him that evening.

Kim was still feeling uneasy about Fresh, and she was surprised to find out who it was driving the black car. "Jade, you told me that night at the restaurant that he'd find you again, and to think, I was all goo-goo eyed over him.

"Girl, he was trying to play us big time. You'd better watch out for him too. Something's not right there. And be careful with Fresh. I don't care how many years of college he's had – I still don't believe he's being straight with you either."

Jade was a little annoyed by what Kim was saying. She seemed to be questioning her ability to do her job. But that was Kim – whatever came up would usually come out.

Jade had to admit it herself; she too had thought Fresh was holding back something. She knew she didn't like or trust Lee, because she had bad vibes about him.

She would have to handle him differently than Fresh. After seeing him that evening, she would know exactly what to do.

Jade changed the subject. She wanted to know how Kim's date went with Phillip. "So, are you going to tell me about lunch or not?"

Kim sounded excited, and said, "Jade, I'm in love."

She talked on and on about Phillip until Jade had to finally cut her off.

Jade decided to get on her computer for a while. She grabbed a bottle of water out of her empty refrigerator, and a bag of chips out of the cabinet.

When Jade finally looked at the clock on her computer, she realized that it was nearing the time for her to visit with Lee. It was seven – thirty, and she had been on the computer for several hours.

Jade had mixed emotions about being alone with Lee in his house. She couldn't put her finger on it, but there were definitely evil vibes abounding.

She fixed her a cup of tea and sat down to map out her strategy. Lee was smart and calculating, so she would have to handle him carefully.

Jade pulled into his driveway, and drove up to the garage doors. She didn't see his car, but she assumed he had parked it in the garage.

She got out of her car, and walked to the front door – but before she rang the doorbell, she looked around the front yard. It was eerily quiet, and she thought about the old man she had seen in the yard the day before.

Jade took a deep breath and asked herself if she really wanted to do this. Just then, the door opened, and Lee was standing there with a drink in his hand. He was wearing a black silk shirt, and black slacks. She tried to block out, how handsome he looked.

"Well hello, I thought I heard you pulling up. Come on in," Lee said, as he opened the door. "You look nice Jade, I like those jeans," he said, as she walked passed him.

Jade was wearing a white top with her jeans and had on a short black leather jacket, and black leather boots.

As Jade walked in, she immediately started looking around. She could tell Lee had expensive taste, judging from the type of clothes he wore, the car he drove, and now looking at the type of furniture he had in his house.

It was decorated in contemporary fashion. The living room walls were painted in a dark salmon color, adorned by large expensive black art paintings, with an over sized white Scandinavian sofa and chair. Salmon and teal pillows were tossed about, completing the furnishings. Large potted plants occupied the corners of the room, along with glass – top tables, and crystal lamps.

Lee led her into the den, and poured her a glass of chilled chardonnay. He remarked, "I remembered you drinking this at the restaurant."

"How thoughtful," she responded, as she reached for the glass. "Did you decorate this house? It's very nice."

Then she took a seat at the bar, hoping he would sit elsewhere. He hesitated a moment, obviously wanting her to sit next to him on the black leather sofa.

"Yes I did decorate it – and I'm glad you like it. Would you like to look at the rest of the house?"

Since Lee appeared to be self – centered, Jade decided she would try to keep the attention on him. She would keep him talking about himself to gather any information she could use.

Jade smiled and said, "Yes, I would love to see it."

As they walked from room to room, Jade complimented him on the décor, colors, and furnishings. She also asked as many questions as possible to keep his mind on the house – and not on her.

Occasionally, he would try to make advances toward her, but she brushed them off. Jade's indifference was disturbing to him. He was used to having his way with women.

"Tell me something, Lee. Obviously, you are financially well-off, judging from your surroundings. So what type of work do you do?" Jade asked coyly.

"I'm into financing," he said.

"Oh really? Do you work at a bank?" Jade asked.

Lee laughed and replied, "A bank? Are you serious? I *own* a business, and I don't work for nobody. I am the boss!"

"I'm impressed, Mr. Anderson. What's the name of your business?" she inquired.

"LA & Associates Mortgage Company," Lee answered proudly. "We make loans for home renovations and repairs. You need a loan?"

They both laughed and Jade continued to probe, "How many associates do you have, or are you in business alone?

Lee frowned, and asked, "Why is that important to you?"

Jade decided to leave that alone, and she asked another question, "I assume that the initials on both your mailbox and business stand for Lee Anderson."

Just then the telephone rang, and Lee answered. "Hello? I told you I was having company – and not to call me until later," then he hung up.

Lee's entire disposition changed. He looked at Jade intensely, and said, "It's not wise for you to assume, you know that, don't you? May I refresh your drink?"

Jade noticed his irritation with her – or whoever had just called – and she knew it was time to go. She wasn't sure what had pissed him off, and she really didn't care – but he was obviously mad about something.

She looked at her watch, it was ten o'clock. She had been there, two hours – too long.

"Don't worry about refreshing my drink Lee, I really have to go. Thank you for your hospitality, and the tour of your beautiful home," Jade said as she grabbed her purse, and headed for the door.

Lee wasn't ready for her to go. He grabbed her arm and asked, "Why are you leaving so soon? Was it the phone call? Don't worry about that, baby – everything is under control!"

Jade tried to pull her arm away, but he gripped tighter. "Excuse me, but you're hurting my arm," she said.

"I assumed we were going to spend some time together, Ms. Lewis," Lee said angrily.

Jade jerked her arm away from him and responded, "It's not wise for you to assume, Mr. Anderson. Good night!" She walked quickly to the door, and out to her car.

After Jade left, Lee had another drink and smoked a joint. He was pissed off and mad. *Women just don't walk out on me!* He thought. Just then his doorbell rang and he got up to see who it was, "I thought I told you to call me first, – but since you're here, come on in. Lee shut the door.

CHAPTER VII

THE SCOOP

It was Friday morning, and it was going to be a busy day for Jade. She had to meet with Sean and Bob at ten, and in spite of her pleas with the receptionist at Tee's Hair Salon for a later appointment time, she was scheduled for eleven.

She also had to prepare for her dinner date with Brian. She wanted to look extra special, so she had planned to go shopping for a new outfit after she left the salon.

Jade had not jogged for the past two days. She needed to absorb the events she had encountered during the earlier part of the week.

Jade had met with Scooter the day before, at the coffee house in the village. He had taken some pictures, and wanted her to look at them. Scooter had taken some shots of all the properties that

were being renovated in the Waverly Park community. He even had pictures of the building where, LA Mortgage and Associates had an office.

"These are very good shots, Scooter. Nice work," Jade said as she looked over the pictures.

"Tank yah, Ms. Jade. Now, tek a look at dis. Dey look rada *interesting!"*

He handed her a stack of pictures. As Jade sipped on a cup of cappuccino, she began looking at the pictures.

They were shots of Lee, and two other men, at night – standing in the parking lot of the building. It appeared that Lee was taking packages, wrapped in brown paper, from the trunk of his BMW. Scooter captured a couple of shots, showing – Lee handing the packages to the two men.

"Hmm," sighed Jade. "What do you think are in those packages?"

"Ah, Ms. Jade, from de look of it's size, ahn shape. I would say it to be, drugs or money. Yuh see de vehicle in de picture-also, Mo Jade?" Scooter asked, pointing to a silver range rover.

Jade stared momentarily, and inquired, "Is that what the men are driving?"

"Yeh mon, it is," replied Scooter.

He pointed out the heavy-set man as the driver. He also gave Jade the license plate number, he had obtained, while following them. Jade thanked Scooter and complimented him, on a job well done.

Jade tracked down the license number. It was registered to Juan Gonzalez. Jade would ask Fresh about him.

Today, Jade felt the need to go out and run.

Just then the telephone rang, "Hello?" she asked. The other line went dead.

Jade had just started receiving these telephone calls. Someone kept calling and hanging up. She was unable to trace the number, it always came up as private, on her caller I.D.

She had her suspicions it was either Fresh or Lee – and she had planned to confront them today.

On her way out, she saw Mama Jo in the swing, on her front porch, “Hey Mama Jo, how are you doing this morning?”She asked.

Mama Jo smiled, and waved at Jade. “Fine Baby, where you been? I haven’t seen you lately.” Jade walked upon the porch.

She informed her she was working on a story, and had been busy. She promised to visit with her after she got back from her hair appointment.

Jade didn’t want to tell Mama Jo she had attempted several times to visit her, but had heard Jennifer and her arguing.

“Where are you on your way to?” Jade asked Mama Jo, as she gave her a big hug.

“Jennifer is taking me to the grocery store, I’m waiting on her now,” Mama Jo said.

“Okay, I’ll see you later,” Jade said, as she ran down Montrose.

Fresh was not at the corner house being renovated. She asked the foreman if he had seen him, and she was informed Fresh was out of town.

Jade asked how long he'd been gone, and she was told he left the day before. She was trying to figure out who had been calling her by the process of elimination.

As she ran further down the street, she saw Lee getting something out of the mailbox; she stopped and asked if she could speak with him.

He was very sharp with her, and asked, "What do you want Jade? I'm real busy."

Jade was thrown off by his tone of voice, and didn't feel comfortable about accusing him of calling her. *After all,* she thought, *how could he have gotten my number?*

At this point, she couldn't prove if it was him, so she decided to play it off.

"Lee, I just wanted to apologize for leaving so abruptly the other night – but you were moving a little too fast for me." Jade wanted to smack herself for allowing those words to come out of her mouth, but she didn't know what else to say.

Her statement certainly got his attention, but his demeanor changed only slightly. He acted as if she owed him – and now it was time to pay.

"So what are you saying? Look Jade, I'm a very busy man, and I don't have time to play. You'll just have to call me later, to see if I can fit you into my schedule," he said arrogantly.

Jade was shocked to hear him say that, and thought, *Oh, no he didn't!*

"Let me tell you something, Lee. You may be able to talk to other women like that – but not here, buddy!" Jade said defiantly.

Just then Jennifer and Mama Jo drove down the street. Jade threw up her hand to wave, but they kept going. She thought Jennifer had seen her, and turned away – but maybe she was mistaken.

Lee was still talking, but Jade wasn't paying any attention. She decided she didn't need him to get the information. It wasn't worth the trouble.

He continued to speak, "Take my number down and call me later."

Jade looked at him and coolly asked, "Call you for what? I really don't have the time or the interest." She turned to continue her run, feeling good about the decision she had made.

She despised Lee and didn't feel like pretending anymore!

Lee was agitated; he hated being rejected by her.

He grabbed Jade and picked her up. She began kicking, and screaming, but he overpowered her.

He took her to his house, and pushed her through the front door. She fell and cut her arm.

"What are you doing? Look at my arm! It's bleeding! I don't know what you have in mind, but it's not happening here," Jade said, as she tried to stop the bleeding.

Lee was breathing hard and his eyes appeared to bulge from their sockets. He remained silent as he pushed her throughout the house, until they reached his bedroom. He then tossed her on the bed, and stood over her.

Jade looked at his nightstand. She was looking for something to hit him with, when she noticed a razor blade laying in a white powdery substance. She immediately recognized it as cocaine.

Lee saw her staring at the table, and asked, "Would you like some Jade, is this what you want, would this make you feel better about me?"

He leaned over to the table, and put some of the cocaine on his finger, and sniffed it. Then he grabbed Jade by her ponytail and attempted to push her face into the powder.

Jade resisted. Lee's behavior was violent and erratic. He was too strong to fight off, so she needed to think of something quick to divert his attention. She knew she had to get out of there – and get out soon – before he hurt her.

As he struggled to push her face down on the table, and into the cocaine, Jade could hear him saying, "You gonna make love to me, you won't walk out of here this time."

Jade responded as calmly as she could make herself. "Lee, take it easy, stop Lee please. If that's all you want to do, then why didn't you say so? I don't need cocaine in order to make love. Let me go and I'll show you."

Lee loosened his grip on her, and she was able to raise her head. She showed him the bleeding wound on her arm, and said, "Look, this blood is dripping everywhere – and I don't want to get it on your bedspread. Blood stains you know. Before we get started, will you get me a towel to wipe it off – and wet it please?"

Lee looked at her with wild eyes, and said, "Okay, I'll get a towel, but don't move girl, don't make me hurt you."

When he left the room, Jade picked up the razor blade and hid it in between her fingers. When Lee came back into the room with the towel, Jade continued to try to keep him calm. She commented on how well his gardener kept the yard, and she told him she had met him the other day.

This seemed to have upset Lee and he screamed at her, "What in the hell are you talking about Jade? I don't have a gardener. I do my own yard. What you trying to do, make me think I'm crazy?"

Jade was surprised to hear that, but she didn't want to lose focus. Lee was becoming more erratic, and she panicked.

As he handed her the towel, she grabbed it with her left hand and then she raised her right one and swung it across his forehead and eyebrow. As the razor blade connected with his skin, she dug deeper into it, and dragged the razor across his eyebrow until the blood began to spill out. It blinded him, and he put his hand over his eye, trying to stop the blood from running into it.

Jade dropped the blade and summoned up as much energy as she could. She ran through the house to the front door. Lee was trailing her, and when she reached the door, he tried to grab at her but – he couldn't see. She swatted him across the eye with the wet towel. This stung and startled him. He jumped back, and let out a yell, "You bitch! Look at what you've done to my face! You'll pay for this!"

Jade was able to escape, while Lee ran to the bathroom, to check on his eye.

Jade didn't stop running until she reached her front door. She was exhausted and still shaken from what had happened to her.

Jade was suppose to meet with Sean and Bob in an hour, but she couldn't, she was still too nervous – and she didn't think she could conceal her emotions from them.

She called Sean, and asked if they could reschedule the meeting. She pretended to have a migraine headache.

"I hope you feel better Jade. You don't sound too good – are you sure you're okay?" Sean asked probingly.

"I'll be okay, I've taken some aspirins, and I'm going to lie down for a minute," Jade said. "Will you explain this to Bob for me? I'll call you Monday morning."

Jade was afraid if they found out what had happened to her, she would be taken off the story – and no matter how much Lee had frightened her, she was not going to let that happen.

She decided to lie down before her next appointment.

After Jade got up, she showered, and dressed, then she left for her hair appointment.

Jade drove slowly towards the Village, which was a very unique area. It was attractive to the thirty – something crowd, the academic community, students, musicians, artists and long – time residents.

All the old – buildings had been renovated. The multi-ethnic restaurants were decorated according to the culture or cuisine, as were the boutiques and other specialty shops.

The lunch crowd was beginning to fill up the restaurants, and finding a parking space would be difficult. As Jade drove further down the street, she noticed a very bright colored sign. T's

URBAN REFLECTIONS hair salon was painted in various shades of pink, turquoise, brown and taupe.

There were painted head models reflecting a variety of urban hairstyles located on a huge glass window.

Jade spotted a parking space within feet of the hair salon. She quickly pulled into it, locked her car doors, and headed into the salon.

Inside, was immaculate. It was decorated in animal print décor, very urban, very chic. There were ten operators, six-black male and females, four-white male and females, one receptionist, two hair washers and four manicurists. They served a diverse clientele.

Jade thought, *not bad for an ex-stripper, Tee really put this place together; I wonder who her benefactor is?*"

The receptionist was very professional, and spoke politely.

Jade gave her name, and she entered it into the computer. The stylist's name came up. She then sent a signal to Tee, who had a small computerized board at her station, alerting her, her appointment, had arrived.

"Have a seat and your stylist will be here momentarily. Would you like something to drink – a soda, water, or wine?" she asked.

Jade declined, and looked around for a seat. She was tired and needed to sit down and try to relax her mind. She was trying hard to forget about what had happened to her earlier.

The reception area was crowded, but Jade spotted a seat next to a middle – age black woman, who had a turban on her head.

Jade couldn't help but notice how aloof the woman appeared. There was a sadness about her; she looked as if she was carrying the weight of the world on her shoulders. As Jade sat down, she looked over at the woman and smiled. The woman gave Jade a quick smile and nod. She stared at Jade for a moment, and then she retreated back into her own space.

Just then, someone called out Jade's name. It was Tee, and as Jade walked over to her, Tee hugged her and said, "Hey girl, Kim said you were going to call. How have you been? I haven't seen you in a while."

She lifted Jade's hair up, and continued, "Look at all this hair! You letting it grow out? It looks nice, and feels healthy. What kind of style are you looking for?"

"I'm not sure what I want to do with it, but I need something that's carefree. I was wearing twists, but this new guy I met likes it like this, what do you think?" Jade asked.

They walked over to the station, and Jade sat down in the chair. Tee told the girls who wash hair she would take care of Jade's head, this would give them more time to talk.

"Girl, if you got a man that pays attention to you long enough to know what your hair looks like, then you'd better stick with that style and stick with that man."

They laughed and gave each other a high-five. Tee, was short for Tiara Smith – a twenty-eight – year old ex – stripper, and a Janet Jackson look-a-like, with a body to match. She had lived life in the fast lane ever since her early teens.

Tee was real, and had an award – winning personality. A really smart girl, she just happened to make the wrong choices in men and in some life decisions. She was a survivor who used what she had to get what she wanted.

"Tee, I am so proud of you, look at how you worked this shop, girl. You got it going on up in here. I know it's none of my business – but I'm going to say it anyway. I'm so glad you stopped

dancing, you're too good for that type of life. You are a beautiful person – inside and out," Jade said sincerely.

Tee responded, "Girlfriend, the only dancing I do now is at home when I exercise. But, I really appreciate what you just said, thank you Jade. I had to stop. It was time. I go to church now, and girl, can you believe I sing in the choir? If it hadn't been for my boyfriend, I don't know what I would have done.

"This is his building, you know? He had it fixed up for me, but I decorated it, and hired all the people – and I collect and keep all the money."

"I heard that," Jade said. "And as they say, 'Don't work for the money, let the money work for you.' So invest, and bank that money, honey."

Some of the operators and patrons overheard Jade's remark, and were amused by it.

Tee decided what she was going to do with Jade's hair, and she explained, "Jade, how about I just clip your ends? I think this length is becoming on you, and I'll perm it to knock out some of these waves, wrap it, and put you under the dryer. You think you'll like that?"

"Sounds good to me and as long as it's carefree," Jade responded.

As Tee began perming Jade's hair, she asked her about the story she was writing on the Waverly Park Community. Jade explained she was doing a feature story on a man named Lester Albright who was killed mysteriously.

Jade asked Tee to tell her all she knew about him, and got her permission to tape the conversation, she would not be named.

Tee said some of this information was from hearing her mother, and others in the neighborhood talk-but she had some encounters with Albright.

"Lester was a low – down dog." Tee said. He pretended to be helping people out, but he didn't mean them no good. He would solicit business from these poor people by going to their houses, and convincing them that they needed work done.

He told them he could save them a lot of money in the long run if they would take out a loan from him. He would charge high interests rates, because most of them couldn't get credit nowhere else, so they ended up paying back double the amount they borrowed. Half of them lost their homes –to him.

"Some of them couldn't read, and they would take him at his word. They trusted him, and would go ahead and sign the papers. He would foreclose on some people, and then put their houses up for sale. Others he foreclosed on, he would continue to let them stay there – and charge them rent.

"I know you heard about the foreclosure on this little old black couple's house. Girl, *everybody* got mad.

"They were the sweetest people you ever wanted to meet, and he just took their house. This killed them, I mean literally killed them.

"It was so sad. He had a lot of people fooled, but when this happened, even those that liked him, got mad.

"The association filed a lawsuit – and girl, that's when they found the fool dead, in his car. Somebody had shot him twice in the heart.

To this day, nobody knows who killed him – or least they ain't telling.

"Nobody cared either; they didn't even mind dropping the lawsuit. They got their justice.

"When I was about fifteen or sixteen, he would always see me walking, and would try to get me to get in his car. Well, one day I did. It was raining and he offered me a ride – but he wouldn't take me home. He drove to the park instead.

"When he stopped the car, he was grabbing on me, and trying to kiss me. Girl, I tried to bite his lip off – and then I hit him upside the head with his briefcase. I jumped out of the car, and Lester Albright never tried to pick me up again.

You know he liked black women – and was always trying to screw them. He didn't care what age they were.

"I had heard that some lady killed herself because of him. She was working for him and all of a sudden, they say she committed suicide. Some people say they had a child together. A girl. And you know, he's got a son too, but he's by another black lady – and I don't know who they are. My mother was president of the association at that time. You need to call her. She can tell you a lot more about the scumbag."

Jade almost fell out of the chair because of what she had just heard. Tee thought Jade was burning from the chemicals in her head when she jumped.

"Are you all right? Is this perm burning your head?" Tee asked, nervously.

Jade turned to Tee and responded, "No, no, I'm fine – but tell me what did you just say? Who committed suicide, and who had a baby by Lester? I'm sorry, Tee, but could you please repeat this again and slowly." Tee repeated to Jade just what she had previously said, but she wasn't sure who these people were or where they were.

"My mother knows about this, just call her. I'm going to tell her, you will be calling."

Jade clicked off the tape recorder, thanked Tee for her help, and promised to call her mother. After Tee finished with Jade's hair, it was beautiful. She really liked the way it just hung down her back, and flowed full of body.

Everybody in the shop complimented her, and when Jade paid, she tipped Tee extra – not only for the hairstyle but for the information as well.

Before Jade left, she asked nervously, "Tee, I've got one more question. Do you know the guy who lives in the Albright house now?"

"I've met him, his name is Lee, he and my boyfriend are in business together – but he really don't trust him. He thinks that he is beating him out of some profits – but he can't prove it. He's fine Jade, but girl he is crazy – and he thinks he's all that. My boyfriend said he likes to beat on woman too."

Jade asked suspiciously, "Who's your boyfriend Tee?"

Tee started grinning from ear to ear and answered, "His name is Fresh – Fredrick Douglas, III. Have you met him yet? Girl he would have a fit over you! He likes to flirt, and he's always on Montrose. You'll know him when you see him."

Jade took a deep breath; she didn't want to tell her she had already met Fresh.

She didn't want her to know just how flirty he had been with her.

"No, I haven't met him yet, but he must be special. It looks like he makes you very happy, and I'm glad for you."

Then Jade hugged her friend and left.

Jade had just gotten the scoop from Tee, that she needed, however she wasn't that excited. She was feeling a little melancholy, and she didn't know why.

She thought perhaps it was because all the events that had transpired thus far, and everything was becoming so real to her now.

Before, it was just names and situations, but now she was able to put faces with the names, the real life, to the situations.

***So much to process,* she thought, and yet there also seemed to be a connection with everybody. It was mind –boggling, like a giant puzzle, and Jade would have to piece it all together.**

Her head was spinning. Too many thoughts were running loose. Every time she thought about what Lee had tried to do to her today, she became more frightened – and she wondered if she had heard him correctly when he said that he didn't have a gardener. *If that was the case, who was the man she spoke with in the yard?*

Jade knew that she should tell somebody about Lee – but who? Who could she trust enough, but wouldn't interfere?

There was also the situation about Nikki. *Could Albright really be the father of her child, instead of Bob – is that why she killed herself?*

This was too confusing to her. She couldn't concentrate, so she would just try to dismiss everything until tomorrow. She has a date that night, a date she had needed for a very long time.

Jade didn't feel like shopping, so she stopped by Mama Jo's, as she had promised. When she rang the doorbell, Jennifer answered it. She appeared to be upset, and didn't say anything to Jade. She just turned around, and retreated to her room. Mama Jo was sitting at the dining room table, motioning for Jade to come in.

Jade was very curious about Jennifer's behavior, and asked Mama Jo, "What's wrong with her?"

Mama Jo looked very tired, and she spoke at a whisper, "I really don't know what's wrong with her. For the past few days, she has been in those dark moods – and I can't say nothing to her. "Just give her some time, and she'll be her normal self again, it's just her ways."

"Would it be all right if I go in there and talk to Jennifer? I would like to help her. Jennifer has some serious issues that need addressing, and it's more to it than just her ways – or moods

Mama Jo. She might need some professional help, have you ever considered that?" Jade asked with obvious concern.

Mama Jo smiled at Jade, patted her on the hand and said, "Now don't you go getting yourself all upset and worried about Jennifer. Trust me, she'll be all right.

"Now let's talk about you, and this big night you got planned. You know, I think Brian is such a nice young man. He's always been sweet to me, and very respectable. I like him, and I hear he likes you too," she chuckled.

Jade blushed, and responded, "Oh really? And who did you hear that from Mama Jo? Never mind – don't tell me, I'm just glad to hear it, because I like him a lot too."

Jade noticed Mama Jo peering at something in the living room. It was Jennifer. She was sitting on the sofa with a blank stare on her face. Jade wondered how long she had been sitting there, and how much had she heard them say.

There was weird silence, when all of a sudden Jennifer blurted out, "I sure hope you treat Brian right Jade. "He's a very nice guy."

This outburst startled and surprised both Jade and Mama Jo. Jade felt compelled to respond. She thought this would be a good opportunity to get Jennifer to talk.

"I don't know what you mean by that remark Jennifer, but I really do like Brian – and I was glad to hear that he likes me, too. I'm really looking forward to tonight."

Jennifer didn't respond, so Jade got up from the table, and walked into the living room.

She picked up Jennifer's baby photo, and asked, "Is this you Jennifer?"

Jennifer got up from the sofa, and walked over to the table where Jade was standing. She picked up each photo, and she calmly responded, "Yes this is me, and this is Kevin. This is Uncle Phillip. This is Granddaddy, and Grandma, and this is their daughter.

Now, is there anything else you want to know, Ms. Psycho analyst?"

By that time Mama Jo had walked into the living room where the girls were standing.

She pointed one finger at Jennifer – and the other at the photo, and said, "Yes, this is my daughter – and she's also your mother. Let me tell you something, chile, no matter what happened, you can't change that fact. You apologize to Jade for being so smart – mouth. She's only trying to be helpful Jennifer."

Jade decided to leave. She felt they needed this moment. Clearly something was going on Jade didn't understand, and she's had enough drama, for one day.

"That's okay, Mama Jo. No apology is necessary. I need to be leaving anyway," Jade said, as she hugged Mama Jo and Jennifer, who just stood there motionless.

Jade had a couple of hours to kill before it was time for her date. She decided to listen to some music, and try to relax, so she popped in a Luther Vandross CD.

As she was curled up on the sofa, she looked out the window, and saw Lee's black car slowly going up the street. Immediately she panicked, and thought about what Tee had said about Lee being crazy.

She knew he would come after her again – after all she had sliced his prize possession – his face. She needed to figure out, how she could stop him.

In spite of her fears, Jade still felt the need to continue her pursuit. She felt there was something else going on besides inflated loans – and she needed to get inside that office to find out what it was. She wanted to hang Lee.

For whatever reason, Jade believed she could trust Fresh, even though she had been warned not to. But she needed him, and would somehow solicit his help.

Jade's phone rang, but she refused to answer it. She didn't feel like talking, and decided to let the voice mail pick up. It was another hang – up call, but she wasn't going to stress it.

Brian picked Jade up promptly at seven. He had asked her earlier to decide on a place to eat, and she chose the Bohemian restaurant she had heard about in the Village.

The evening was going very well. Everything felt right for both Jade and Brian, and she was feeling relaxed as she sat with Brian drinking Bahama – Mama's, while he drank rum and coke.

It was a beautiful October evening, though slightly chilly. They decided to have dinner out on the veranda, and it was a very romantic setting.

The tables were adorned with several multiple – size lighted candles whose flames were dancing in the shadow of a full October moon.

Jade had worn a two – piece, black knit skirt set. She accessorized the off-the-shoulder knit top, and straight ankle length skirt with a wide, brown leather belt that encircled her tiny waist. She also had on black and brown Italian, leather boots.

Her freshly done hair was hanging down her back, and blowing in the wind.

Brian was wearing a charcoal – color lambs – wool suit coat, with a black crew neck sweater and black knit slacks.

They were a very handsome couple. Brian looked into Jade's eyes as if he was piercing her soul.

He held her hand and said, "Jade you look so beautiful and sexy tonight."

Jade blushing, responded, "Thank you Brian, you look very handsome yourself."

As the night went on they discussed many topics. Jade had promised him she would tell him about the assignment she was working on. Brian was intrigued by what she was saying and he was amazed at how much information Jade had acquired.

He knew about Fresh, but had never heard of Lee. He also confirmed Kim's suspicion about Fresh selling drugs. He informed her that Fresh was in the big leagues.

"Jade, you are just a little Colombo, aren't you? I've been a detective for six years and I'm not sure I could keep up with you. But seriously Jade, you have got to be careful," Brian said.

Jade sat there for a moment contemplating whether to tell Brian about Lee. She needed to tell somebody in case he came after her again.

"Brian, I need to tell you something and I need your advice."

Brian noticed the concern on Jade's face and asked, "What is it, Baby, what's going on?"

Jade hesitated and then began to speak slowly, "I told you Lee was in partnership with Fresh, but I can't figure out what other role he plays. He's tied in with Albright in some way.

"I say that because he was the one who had LA & Associates Mortgage company originally, and asked Fresh to go in with him. He's also living in Albright's old house.

"After I found out, who he was, I saw him in front of his house one day, and decided to visit – just to see what information I could get out of him. He apparently thought I was there for other reasons and—"

Brian abruptly asked, "What did he do to you Jade?"

Tears filled her eyes, and she began telling Brian how she had walked away the first time; however the next time he forced her into the house, where she fell and cut her arm. She continued to tell him what had transpired after that, and how she had cut him across the face to get out of there.

She told Brian that Lee was self – centered and cocky-and because she messed up his face, he vowed to get her.

Brian reached across the table, and wiped her eyes with his handkerchief. His heart went out to her, and he was furious about what Lee had done.

He asked, "Can I see your arm, how bad is it?"

Jade had put a band aid on it, but she rolled up her sleeve, and took it off to show Brian the cut.

"Ironically, this is what saved me. I used it as a diversion tactic to help me get out of there – and it worked," Jade said.

Brian shook his head, and smiled slightly before responding, "Girl, I don't know what I'm going to do with you, you could have gotten yourself killed or hurt, but I have to give it to you, you are one determined young lady. I want you to press charges against him for assault, and I'll handle the rest."

"I can't press charges, it would bring too much attention, and I'd be off the story," Jade said, sadly.

"Don't worry about it. Just let me handle him, I'll take care of it," Brian said.

Jade felt so much better. She was glad she had trusted Brian – she felt comfortable in talking with him.

"You had asked me about Lester Albright. I didn't know him personally, but Phillip told me about him. Phillip hated this man's guts," Brian said.

Jade was curious, and asked, "Oh really? Why did Phillip hate him so much?"

"Jade, you don't know?" Brian asked, hesitantly.

"Know what Brian," she asked.

Brian realizing, she didn't know what he was talking about, hesitated to tell her.

"Never mind, I guess everybody hated Lester, he certainly did enough to make people feel that way,"

Brian hoped that was the end of it. But Jade, being persistent as she was, did not give in so easily, "Tell me, Brian, what are you talking about?" Jade prodded.

Brian became very serious and said, "I just assumed that you knew, especially since you were working on the story. Look – what I'm about to tell you is something that has caused this family, a lot of pain. So please don't say anything.

"Phillip's sister committed suicide years ago and it had something to do with Lester Albright. She was Jennifer and Kevin's mother."

Jade was shocked. Finally she was able to utter a few words, "You mean Nikki is Phillip's sister? Jennifer and Kevin are Nikki's children? Mama Jo is, Oh – my – God!"

Brian was confused and asked, "So you did know about Nikki?"

"No, no – I mean yes – I mean, Brian you are not going to believe this," Jade said, as she went on to explain the part of the investigation she had left out about Bob, Nikki, and how it related to Lester Albright.

CHAPTER VIII

IN TOO DEEP…

As Brian was driving Jade home, she was silent. She kept going over and over in her mind how she had been literally sitting on top of Nikki's family. She didn't understand how she missed the obvious signs. She had become very fond of the family – and perhaps, became too involved to see what was really going on.

***Maybe that's what was going on with Jennifer,* she thought.**

Brian almost wished he had never said anything to Jade about Nikki. Not because he didn't want her to know, but because this news seemed to have darkened her mood.

"Jade, I think you are allowing this to consume too much of you. Take it from one who knows. You can become too deeply involved, and you'll eventually lose sight of everything. I'm going to have to help you slow down," Brian said.

Jade smiled at him and asked, "Just how do you plan to do that, Mr. Williams?"

Brian pulled up in front of Mama Jo's house, and parked his car. He leaned over, put his arms around her and said, "I can show you, better than I can tell you."

Brian walked Jade to her door and she thanked him for a wonderful night.

Neither wanted this night to end, but Brian was meeting some friends to play golf at seven in the morning, and Jade had already planned to interview some people for her story.

"I want you to spend all day Sunday with me. So do all the work you want to on tomorrow – you are definitely off duty Sunday. I've got something specially planned for you.

Now, let me to show you, what I was talking about in the car," Brian said.

When he placed his arms around her, she began to melt, as he leaned closer towards her, she could smell his cologne. Jade looked up at Brian's perfectly – shaped lips, and she instinctively closed her eyes.

He kissed her lightly on the cheek, then he tenderly brushed his mouth against hers. As he parted his lips, she responded as well, and they began to kiss. Jade felt wonderful as she stood there in Brian's arms.

They kissed again; it was long, sensuous, and full of emotion.

Brian took Jade's keys, and opened the door. She could hear the telephone ringing, and told Brian it was probably Kim, but when she answered it, all she could hear was music. Then it clicked off.

Brian could tell from the look on her face this had happened before.

"How long have you been getting these calls, Jade?" he asked.

Jade decided to tell him the truth. "It's been going on for the past three or four days, they call sometimes once a day, twice a day and this makes the third time today. I could be wrong, but I think it might be Lee Anderson calling. He's trying to intimidate me."

Brian didn't want to leave her by herself, he offered to stay and sleep on the day bed, but Jade reassured him she would be okay.

Secretly, she wanted him to stay, she wanted to curl up in bed with him and lay in his arms all night long.

As Jade laid in the bed, the next morning, all she could think about was the wonderful evening, she and Brian had, and how he had kissed her with those sexy lips.

She wasn't sure, but she thought she might be falling in love.

Jade decided not to run that morning. She had work to do, she needed to go over everything she had learned the day before and refocus – plus she was afraid of running into Lee.

Brian had already called her from the golf course, he wanted to make sure she was okay. He asked her not to go near Lee's house, and to be careful, when she was out. He would call her later.

Jade had gotten out of bed, and decided to fix breakfast, when the telephone rang.

"Hello." Jade said, as she picked up the telephone.

It was Kim. She wanted a play-by-play description of Jade's date last night.

"Kim, I had the most wonderful time of my life. Just when you feel all hope is lost, the universe shoots to you, a 'shinning star.' This man is wonderful!" Jade said excitedly.

"Girl, I've got to meet this man, I have never heard you talk like this, before. But, I ain't mad at ya.' You need to enjoy yourself. Answer this one thing-can he kiss?" Kim asked.

"Can he kiss?" Jade repeated. "Are you kidding? Kim, when that man kissed me, I literally felt the porch move, it felt like we were locked in a time zone, and we were spinning through a tunnel."

"It must have been good girl, cause he's got you reciting poetry. I bet Brian's lips are still burning," Kim said teasingly.

After Jade filled her in on the details of her date, they discussed what was going on with the investigation. Kim, out of concern, asked if she could come over to help Jade out today.

She had not told Kim what happened to her with Lee, but she sure welcomed her company.

Jade fixed her a cup of tea, and sat down at her computer. She wanted to call Sean and tell him about Jennifer, but she decided not to until she was able to find out more information.

She pulled Mrs. Smith's telephone number Tee had given her, out from her purse. She decided to start with her first.

"Hello, may I speak with Mrs. Smith please, this is Jade Lewis," Jade said, as Mrs. Smith answered the phone.

She told Jade she was expecting her call and began to tell her about Lester Albright, much of it the same information that she had already heard.

Jade then asked, "Did you know Nikki Johnson, the lady that committed suicide?"

Mrs. Smith answered eagerly, "Yes I did, she's Josephine Johnson's daughter. That was so sad, but that Lester drove her to do that, I just know he did.

"I don't know why she went to work for him, because the girl was a registered nurse, but I had heard it had something to do with paying off a loan. She was a beautiful girl, very smart, and sweet. She would do whatever she could for you.

"They say Jennifer is his daughter, and since she is mixed, she probably is his. Nikki wasn't seeing anybody else at that time."

"Nikki wasn't involved with anyone as far as you know Mrs. Smith – but she could have been seeing someone else," Jade interrupted.

Jade knew she had been. She was having an affair with Bob, a white man, therefore Jennifer would be biracial either way, but Jade couldn't tell Mrs. Smith that.

"I guess you are right, baby, but I'll tell you someone who knows a whole lot more than I do – and her name is Peggy. She was fooling around with Lester Albright too, and they say she had a boy by him. I think that child died or something because nobody has ever seen him. She and Nikki knew each other very well. Give her a call and tell her that I gave you the number, she won't mind," Mrs. Smith gave her the telephone number and Jade thanked her for her time.

When Jade got off the phone, she thought about how this story was becoming more and more bizarre each time she received new information.

Peggy would be the person who could shed light on some of these unanswered questions, **Jade thought.** ***That is, if she would be willing to talk.*** **She also wanted to know the real circumstances behind Peggy and Nikki's friendship – since they both supposedly had affairs and children with Albright. She was confused, but hoped that Peggy could help make some sense of this situation.**

She realized, she didn't have Peggy's last name – but she dialed her number, anyway. The phone rang for a while before someone answered.

"Hello," a female voice on the line said.

Jade cleared her throat and said, "Hi, my name is Jade Lewis. Is Peggy in?"

"This is she." Peggy answered.

Jade introduced herself. She proceeded to tell Peggy about the story she was writing on the Waverly Park Community, and how she was profiling Lester Albright, and the circumstances surrounding his mysterious death.

She informed her Mrs. Smith had given her name as a reference. Peggy was a little hesitant at first but then she decided to allow Jade to come by her house to interview her. She gave her

the address, which was at the other end of Montrose, and asked her to come at three o'clock.

Jade had another plan in mind regarding Fresh, but she would have to get with Tee today to discuss it. She wasn't sure if Tee was even aware of his drug activities, nor was she sure if she would go along with the plan.

That's where Kim would come in, who could be quite convincing at times. Jade called Tee and explained she had come across some information she might be interested in hearing about Fresh, and she asked if she could meet her for lunch.

Tee checked her calendar, and told her she could meet her at one o'clock. Jade would use the information that she got from Brian to convince Fresh to help her out, along with a little blackmailing.

Jade was feeling herself again. She was making progress, and everything seemed to be falling right into her lap. She thanked God for his divine intervention!

By the time Kim arrived, Jade was ready to go, first they would meet with Tee about Fresh, then Peggy, and last but not

least, she would contact Fresh. Jade had asked Kim not to say anything to Phillip about the investigation and about what Brian had told her. She didn't want to remind them of any more painful memories, at least not yet. Not until she knew definitively who Jennifer's real father was.

Jade and Kim pulled in front of Tee's hair salon. It was a few minutes past one o'clock and it appeared that the shop was near empty. They walked in, and Tee was cleaning up around her station.

"Hey ladies, I'll be finished in a second. Have a seat. Can I get you anything?" Tee asked.

They both declined, and sat down in the lobby area, to wait on Tee.

Some of the other operators had a few customers, and told her they would lock up after they finished. After she had completed her station, Tee freshened up her hair and make-up. She suggested they walk down to the Sunset Grille restaurant for lunch.

When they were seated, Tee full of curiosity, asked Jade, "What is this all about, I thought that you didn't know Fresh."

Jade had already prepared for this question, she knew Tee would ask – and she would try to keep it as close to the truth as possible. However she planned to leave out the part where Fresh tried to hit on her. She would use that to convince Fresh to help her out.

Jade responded, "I really don't know him Tee, but I had met him on Montrose while I was out jogging and I wasn't sure what his name was. We talked briefly about his construction business, and how he got started.

"He told me he had a partner named Lee, and that's why I asked you about him. I think he has something to do with Lester Albright."

Kim noticed Jade was struggling, and unable to make her point, so she interrupted, "Look Tee, let's get to the point. Fresh is selling drugs, and the information that Jade received, leads her to believe that he and Lee are somehow laundering the profits through their business. She doesn't want you to get messed up with it, and lose your shop. Do you know anything about it?"

Jade stared at Kim, and asked, "Did you have to be so blunt? I was getting there."

"Yeah, when? Tomorrow sometime? Girl, I was just trying to move this thing along, and keep it real." Kim retorted.

"Well, thank you," Jade said sarcastically.

Tee, was watching the both of them in amusement, then she asked Jade, "Suppose I do know a little something, but tell me, where are you going with this?"

Jade agreed to let her in on the plan she had devised against Lee that would put him out of business, but she needed Fresh's help.

Tee told them Fresh was still dealing, but she didn't like it. She was more than willing to help out, and she would go along with anything that would scare him into stopping.

However, she didn't want him involved in anything that would jeopardize his life – and she didn't want him in trouble with the law.

She had told Fresh many times Lee was bad news. Although he didn't trust Lee himself, and have wanted to cut ties with him for a long time, he never made a move. She thought this would be a good opportunity.

Jade went back over her plans with Tee. She told her what she was trying to do, and what she needed to find out.

Tee wanted to help Jade out, and began telling her what she knew about Fresh and Lee's operation.

Jade showed her the pictures, Scooter had taken of the men in the parking lot with Lee.

"Tee, take a look at these pictures, and tell me if you know these men," Jade asked, as she handed her the pictures.

Tee, took the pictures, and immediately said, "Yes. I've seen them both, once-when they met me and Fresh in the park to drop off a package for Lee."

She pointed to the heavy-set man and said, "This man is Juan Gonzalez, I don't know the other man's name. They are from Mexico, and Jade – you don't want to mess with them. They are very dangerous men!"

"Thanks. I'll keep that in mind," Jade said, as she nodded her head.

After they finished eating their lunch, Jade thanked Tee, again. She told her she would call her about Fresh, next week.

Jade and Kim left. They drove towards Peggy's house. They both talked about the new men in their lives, and possibly taking a vacation together during the holidays.

Jade was happy Kim had come along – and she told her. "Kim, I really appreciate you being here, helping me to try and make sense of what's going on. I know that you are worried about me – and I get nervous too, but something tells me everything will be okay."

"Girlfriend are you kidding?" Kim asked. "This saga gets more interesting by the minute. I wouldn't miss being here for the world. You couldn't pay to see a better movie. But on the real side, Jade you are my best friend – and I want to be here for you."

As they turned on Montrose, Jade saw Phillip, and Brian, standing in front of Mama Jo's house. She immediately pulled over.

"Look Kim, there's Brian with Phillip. He must have just finished his golf game. Well, I guess you'll get to meet him, sooner than you expected," Jade said smiling.

"Damn! That *man is fine,* Jade. No wonder, you're running around here reciting poetry. There's my baby – and he's fine too!" Kim said, as they were getting out of the car.

"There you are. I've been trying to reach you, but your cell phone was turned off. I thought I'd better come over here, and check on you," Brian said as he hugged Jade.

"That's so sweet of you Brian. Thank you," Jade said, as she pulled her cell phone out of her purse. "You were right, it is turned off, and I'd better watch that. Brian, this is Kim. She offered to ride with me today, to keep me company."

Brian extended his hand to Kim. "So, you're Kim? I've heard a lot of good things about you. Nice to meet you."

"Hello Brian. And likewise, I've heard good things about you too!" Kim said, as she shook Brian's hand.

"What's going on Phillip?" Jade asked, as she gave him a hug.

"Everything's cool, baby. Just trying to keep my boy from jumping out of his tree. I tried to tell him, you were okay. What have you done to him, Jade?" Phillip asked, laughing.

They all talked for a few more minutes. Phillip, reminded Kim of their date later on. Jade told Brian, she was on her way to another interview. She would call him when she was finished.

Jade and Kim got into the car and left. They pulled up to the house with the address on the mailbox that Peggy had given Jade. It was a small, but neat white – framed house with a fenced-in yard, it appeared to have been painted recently.

Jade rang the doorbell, and when the door opened she gasped, "You're the lady that I saw at the hair salon, yesterday."

The lady standing in the doorway looked surprised herself, she remembered seeing Jade also.

After what seemed to be several moments, she finally asked them to come in and have a seat. Jade introduced Kim and re-introduced herself. "Do you mind Peggy, if I use my tape recorder?" Jade asked, as she held up the recorder.

Peggy shook her head and said, "No."

Jade began to tell Peggy all about the assignment and what Bob had revealed to her about Nikki.

Jade noticed this woman had the very same empty and sad look on her face. She kept her eyes focused on Jade, and didn't talk very much. She would only respond when asked a question.

Jade was becoming frustrated with her. She felt that she was holding back something.

"Peggy, I'm sorry if I seem to be intruding, but you are the only person that can tell me about Nikki and Lester Albright – and whether he is Jennifer's father or not," Jade pleaded.

Peggy spoke softly, "Nikki thought he was the father, and that's what killed her."

Jade was puzzled and asked, "What do you mean by that's what killed her?"

Peggy continued, "Nikki despised Lester and he constantly threatened her about taking her parents home if the loan wasn't paid off, or if she wouldn't sleep with him. She was in love with Bob. The night Bob told her that he would give her the money when he got back; she went to Lester to tell him that she would be paying off the loan.

"This angered Lester, because he really wasn't interested in the money. He wanted her – and so he raped her that night. He

made her swear not to tell, or he would foreclose on her parent's house regardless. The next day or so, Nikki was fired by old man Winslow, who had found out about the affair – and forbade her to ever see Bob again.

"Nikki's world was falling apart; she was scared, desperate, and needed help. But she didn't know where to turn, so she went back to Lester and asked him for a job. She told him she would pay him monthly, until the loan was paid off.

"She hated working for him, and had decided to quit, when she found out that she was pregnant, she assumed she had gotten pregnant the night Lester raped her, because that was the last time she had been with a man.

"Lester told her that he would take care of her, and would tear up the loan contract of her parents if she would continue to see him. She agreed, but when she delivered, she put the babies up for adoption – and refused to see Lester again. However, later on she went back to work for him, he had lied about tearing up her parent's loan contract."

Jade interrupted, and asked, "How many babies did she have? You said she put the *babies* up for adoption."

Peggy answered, "Nikki gave birth to twins."

Jade and Kim both said at the same time, "Twins?"

Then Jade asked, "What happened after she put them up for adoption – and where is the other twin? Was it a boy or girl?"

Peggy responded, "Nobody has ever said, and I don't know. All I know is she ended up with that one little girl. Nikki never got over Bob and she couldn't live with the fact Lester had raped her, and was the father of her child. She couldn't cope, so she committed suicide. That was easier for her than dealing with reality."

Hearing this infuriated Jade. Even though she knew his history, she still wondered how one man could do so much to so many people.

"Peggy, I understand you had a son by Lester. Where is he – and who do you think killed Lester?" Jade asked.

Peggy answered somberly, "I don't have any children, and I don't know who – nor do I care – killed Lester."

Jade was surprised to hear her say she didn't have any children, but she decided to leave that alone, and prodded further, "Some guys have bought Albright's business, I've met

them both, and it appears they have some of the same business practices as Albright did. I'm not sure how they were able to obtain it, but I think I know how they are running it now. Do you know Lee Anderson or Freddie Douglas?

"Peggy appeared stunned at how much Jade knew. It seemed for one moment she even smiled at Jade as she spoke, "It's amazing, it's truly amazing."

"What's amazing?" Jade interrupted.

Peggy shook her head and said, "Nothing, never mind. You're overlooking one important piece of the puzzle, just look around you Jade, or are you too involved to see. Stop it here, leave well enough alone and write your story."

Then she stood up and walked to the door. Jade got up and asked, "What are you saying Peggy? And what do you mean by, 'leave well enough alone?' What is it? Does it have something to do with Lee and Fresh?"

Peggy said with concern in her voice, "Leave it alone Jade. It's too complicated, and too dangerous, for you to handle. You should leave now."

Jade and Kim left. They were both in awe at the way Peggy had abruptly ended their visit. Jade pulled in front of her house, and Kim got out and into her car. She had to leave, she was meeting Phillip later.

Before Kim pulled off, she said to Jade, "Please be careful when you talk with Fresh. That Peggy woman is a weirdo, she sort of unnerved me with that strange talk-but clearly she was sending you a message."

"You know, I picked up on that too, Kim. She knows something, and she's not telling. She's scared of something. Somehow I'm going to find out what it is," Jade said with conviction.

Jade still had plenty to do. She had one more call to make. She pulled out Fresh's cell phone number, and dialed it.

"Hey Fresh, this is Jade. What's up?"

Fresh was totally shocked, but pleased to hear Jade's voice, "Hey pretty lady, I was looking for you this morning, I heard you been looking for me, but I had to make a little run out of town. You ready to go out with me yet?"

"I don't think Tee would be very happy with that – do you?" Jade asked.

Fresh was startled, but answered, "She won't know if you don't tell. How did you find out about her anyway?"

"Oh. I had a hair appointment with her yesterday and your name came up during our conversation. You know how girls talk when they get together. By the way Fresh, what did you pick up on your little run out of town, yesterday?" She asked.

Jade was bluffing. Fresh was very disturbed, "What are you talking about, and what has Tee been telling you?"

"Now, now, Fresh, let's not get nasty here," Jade said teasingly. "Tee didn't tell me anything. As a matter of fact, I haven't told her anything about you either. I told her that I had met you while I was running. That's all, she is such a nice girl. I just couldn't tell her you were trying to hit on me."

Fresh said sarcastically, "Well aren't you noble, you must want something. Who are you anyway – do you work for the police?"

Jade decided to be straight with him, although he was not someone she wanted to be bothered with, there was still something about him that she trusted and respected.

Jade leveled with him who she was, about the story she was working on, and the plan she had devised that included him.

She told him all about Lee, his following her, attacking her and now calling her house, hanging up. Jade also told him that a police source had given her the information about his drug dealings.

Fresh was surprised, and said, "Girl, you are too good. You played me big time. But you know what; I knew something wasn't right. You asked too many questions.

"Why do you want to help me out anyway? I'm just as guilty as Lee. I'm the one who introduced him into the drug business, I handle the deliveries. If the Police have already told you this, why would you still want to trust me?"

"First of all, I'm going to help you because I need you to help me out," Jade responded. "Secondly, why would you set yourself up to be the fall guy for Lee? I know you're making money – and he is too –but it's at your expense. Third, I trust you because you

trusted me enough to confide in me about how you got started selling drugs – and eventually got into this business.

"I saw how you handle your business with the contractors, and the construction crew. I was impressed. Remember, I complimented you. You showed compassion when you said you didn't like what Lee was doing to some of his clients with the loans and foreclosures. That stuck in my mind."

Fresh, was obviously enjoying the compliments.

"What guarantee do I have that the police will give me protection?" He asked. "These drug people can be mean you know – and how do you know Lee is gooking me?"

"Because – you believe he's gooking you. You've said so, yourself," she responded. Fresh, you know he can't be trusted, look at what he's doing to those innocent homeowners. You know how dangerous he can be; look at what he tried to do to me."

"Yeah man, that's messed up, but Jade, he don't take rejections very well. You need to stay away from him. If he says he's going to get revenge and you have sliced up his pretty face, too! I'd say he's not through with you yet," Fresh said.

Jade responded, "I know, I've been thinking about that. Now look, we need to get off this telephone and meet somewhere to discuss this further. How about I call you tomorrow. I'll have more details about your police protection then, and be thinking about somewhere we can meet that will be safe. I've already been warned how I'm in too deep and how dangerous this could get."

"Warned by who?" Fresh asked.

"By this lady I talked with today named Peggy," Jade answered.

"Who? Ms. Peggy Anderson?" Fresh asked.

Jade wasn't sure what her last name was, but she told Fresh where Peggy lived, and he responded, "That's her and she ought to know. It's her son we're talking about and she definitely knows how dangerous he can be."

Jade was stunned. "You mean to tell me that Lee Anderson is Peggy's son?"

Fresh responded, "Yelp."

CHAPTER IX

THE CONNECTION

Jade was up early. She hadn't sleep well.

She couldn't believe her ears when Fresh told her who Peggy's son was, and she wondered why Peggy had lied about not having children.

Jade was reflecting on everything Peggy had said to them the day before. She couldn't understand why Peggy, on one hand, seemed to be so helpful – and then on the other she was closed mouth.

Why did she talk to them at all? She knew what the investigation was going to be about. Why all the mystery? Now Jade was thoroughly confused.

Jade called Brian and told him about the conversation with Peggy and Fresh. She asked if they could postpone their outing,

but he told her he would be right over, he had something to tell her.

Jade remembered she had told Mama Jo last week she would go to church with her today, but she needed to cancel, she wouldn't be able to concentrate.

She decided to tell her all about the assignment, since she was going to eventually have to tell her anyway. She threw on her sweats, and headed for Mama Jo's.

As Jade was approaching the bottom steps, she noticed something black and furry laying on the last step. The closer she got, she noticed it was a black cat, but it didn't move.

She jumped over it – and when she took a closer look, she screamed. Someone had slit the animal's neck, and blood was running everywhere off the steps.

Jade was hysterical. She couldn't move – all she could do was scream. Mama Jo and Jennifer ran out of the house to where Jade was standing.

Kevin had just pulled up, and he jumped out of his car and ran over to where everyone was standing.

Mama Jo was shocked when she saw the dead cat. She grabbed her chest and said, "My God! Who in the world would do a thing like that? Chile, are you all right? When did this happen?"

Jennifer had put her arms around Jade to calm her down and Kevin found an old blanket in the garage to cover the cat.

"I don't know Mama Jo. It wasn't here last night. I was coming down to tell you that I wouldn't be able to go to church – and there it was." Jade answered through tears.

Phillip and Kim pulled up, they had planned to attend church with Mama Jo also and then Brian pulled in behind them.

Phillip asked as he got out of the car, "What's going on out here?"

Kim saw her friend was crying, and ran up to her. Kim asked if she was okay.

By that time Brian had barely put his car in park before he jumped out, and ran to grab Jade.

"Jade, sweetheart – what's the matter?" He asked. I just talked to you, has something happened?"

"This is what happened," Kevin responded, as he pulled the cover off of the dead cat. "Jade was coming downstairs to Mama Jo's and she found this laying at the bottom of her steps."

Everybody was shocked, and Kim blurted out, "I bet Lee or Fresh did it."

"Who is Lee or Fresh, Baby? Who are these people you're talking about?" Phillip asked.

Kim, realizing she had spoken too soon, apologized, "Jade, I'm sorry, I didn't mean to say anything. I couldn't help it. This is some sick stuff!"

Jade, who was being comforted by Brian, shook her head at Kim, and said, "Don't worry about it Kim, I was planning to tell Mama Jo today anyway. This is getting more serious than I thought, so I'd better let everyone know, about everything."

Brian asked Jade, "Are you sure you want to do this now? You can wait until later."

Mama Jo, obviously upset, asked excitedly, "Will somebody please tell me what's going on?"

Jade decided to tell them while everybody was there. She asked if they could all go into the house. Kevin said he would be in shortly, he was going to dispose of the cat.

Everyone sat down at the dining room table. Jennifer helped Mama Jo to a seat. She felt weak in the knees.

Kevin came in, and Jade began to explain who Fresh and Lee were. She said, she had met them as a result of the story she was working on.

Jade told them Fresh was going to help her to expose Lee, and hopefully put him out of business.

Everyone was silent at first, and then Phillip angrily asked, "Is this the reason why you moved into Mama's house? So you could be close enough to really get the scoop? Are you using my family?

"Why would you drudge up something that happened so long ago? You might not know this, Jade, but my family's been through a lot – and I'm sorry, but I'm not letting you hurt them just to satisfy some newspaper."

Brian interrupted and said, "Hold up man, Jade didn't even know anything about your family. She realized from conversations with Mama Jo you all had been through something

that caused you a lot of hurt. So, she decided not to bother your family with this investigation."

"He's right, Phillip," Kim chimed in. "It was just coincidental that she found this place, she didn't know Mama Jo or any of the family."

"Mama is getting old now, and she can't handle much more, Jennifer said, angrily. "She's been through enough. You just don't understand Jade. Maybe you should just move, and stop messing into people's business – then you won't have to worry about phone calls and dead cats."

Mama Jo responded, "Hush up Jennifer. You hush up now. The girl said she didn't know nothing about this mess. Give her a chance to finish explaining."

Jade stood up. She cleared her throat, and said, "Mama Jo, please believe me when I say I had, no intentions to hurt you or your family. Somehow I see you as an extension of my own family, at least I feel that way.

There is more to this story, than I'm able to talk about, right now. There's a connection. But, I promise you – when all the facts are in – you'll be the first to know. Phillip, whatever the outcome

is, please know, I would never write anything hurtful to your family. I just need you to trust me."

Jade sighed heavily and began telling the story.

"When my boss called me into his office to give me this assignment, and especially after he filled me in on the details, I wanted this story real bad. This man, Lester Albright, seemed like a monster and he had hurt so many people, I wanted to write about it. I wanted to do it for all of the people who are going through the same thing – in other places, and for those who are now being affected, right here – in this neighborhood.

"We weren't even concerned about his murder, or who killed him for that matter. That was not even an issue. I guess what I'm trying to say is, we just don't want Lee to be able to continue what his father had started."

Everybody almost in unison cried out, "His father?"

Jade continued, "Yes, his father. I found out yesterday. Kim and I had visited this lady name Peggy who knew Lester Albright. She was supposed to have had a child by him, but when I asked her, she denied it. I later found out from Fresh, she was Lee's mother. Her name is Peggy Anderson."

"You are kidding, Jade. I told you something was wrong with that woman. She was acting too weird," Kim said, surprised.

"I know, Kim. One thing about it, she knows her son is a dangerous man," Jade said.

All of a sudden Jennifer screamed out, "Liar, liar! What are you trying to do to us? Why do you want to hurt us so much? You are just mad because he didn't want you – so now you want to get even!"

Jade turned to Jennifer, who was crying and hysterical, she attempted to touch her hand – but Jennifer pulled away.

"No Jennifer. You've got it all wrong. He was the one after me." Jade tried to explain.

Then Jade looked at Brian. He nodded.

Jade proceeded to tell them about the day Lee forced her into his house, and about all the things he had done to her.

Kim was shocked and upset Jade had not told her about this. She walked up to Jade, and asked, "Jade, why didn't you tell me? You could have been killed! I begged you to be careful – and you need to stop trying to handle everything all by yourself."

"I know Kim, and you are absolutely right," Jade responded. "You warned me many times to be careful, and I thought I was. I guess I just underestimated the situation."

Jennifer was still crying, so Kevin took her to her room. Jade felt bad for having upset her. She told Mama Jo if she wanted her to move, she would do so.

Mama Jo stood up, and put her arms around Jade, and hugged her. She said, "You will do no such thing. You stay right here, this is your home, chile. And you go ahead, and write your story. Everything's going to be all right. This is something you were sent here to do by divine – order, and you are going to do it."

Mama Jo shouted out, as she walked slowly to her room, "Thank you Jesus! Thank you! Only you know my burdens Lord – and only you can answer my prayers! Thank You!"

Jade and Kim had tears in their eyes, they hugged each other, and then hugged Brian and Phillip.

Kevin hugged Jade and said, "Don't worry about Jennifer; she's going to be okay, and Mama too. She just gets a little choked up sometimes."

They decided to go up to Jade's apartment, but Phillip wanted to check on his mother and niece first, so he told them to go ahead and he would be there shortly.

Jade prepared tea for everybody at her apartment. She had called Fresh, who told her he thought it would be better to meet at her place, and he was bringing Tee with him. He thanked Jade again, for not telling Tee about his flirting with her.

"I wonder why Peggy lied about Lee. Poor Jennifer, I guess it tore her up to think Lee could be her brother," Kim said to Jade.

"No Kim, that wasn't it. Lord knows I hope I'm wrong, but there's something else going on with that," Jade said, as she paced the floor.

Brian and Kim looked at each other, puzzled. Brian asked, "What do you mean Baby, what else do you think is going on?"

Jade hesitated a moment, and then said, "Do you remember hearing Jennifer say if I stayed out of people's business, I wouldn't have to worry about phone calls and dead cats?"

They both agreed they had heard her.

"I never mentioned that I was getting phone calls. No one knew but you two, and I just told Fresh about it yesterday. So how did she know?

"You know, I've seen Jennifer leave at night. Several times – and it's always been late. The first night I went to Lee's house, someone called him and he angrily said to them, 'I thought I told you not to call me until later.'

"After I got home that night, Jennifer immediately got into her car and left. She also saw me standing in front of Lee's house, talking with him on that day he forced me into his house. When I waved to her, as she and Mama Jo passed in the car, she obviously turned away. Ever since then, Jennifer has been acting strange towards me."

Brian put his arm around Jade, and said, "Maybe it's all coincidental, Jade. You have been working too hard on this story, trying to put all the pieces together. You need to relax."

"I don't know Brian, but maybe you are right," Jade said, looking perplexed.

Kim, being in character, responded, "Girl, I hope it is a coincidence – because if it's not, then Jennifer has been sleeping with her brother."

In the back of Jade's mind, she was thinking the same thing. She also wondered if Lee knew who Jennifer really was.

Brian waited on Phillip to join them, before he decided to explain the information he had obtained regarding Fresh's legal dilemma.

When Phillip arrived, Brian began to speak. "Jade, I have some good news and some bad news about Fresh."

Jade appeared concerned. Even though she knew earlier, Brian was coming over with some information, about Fresh. She had a sinking feeling in the pit of her stomach, as she sat down on the edge of her sofa.

Phillip and Kim sat on the other end, as they listened intently.

Brian, who was standing in the middle of the floor, continued to speak. "I've been doing some investigating myself. I found out from Detective Thompson – a friend of mine working narcotics – Phillip, you remember Joe."

Phillip acknowledged, by nodding.

"Well, he told me this case had been picked up by the feds."

"The feds?" interrupted Jade.

"Yes Jade, the feds. This is the bad news. You see the feds have been watching Lee and Fresh for a while. They know about their drug operation, and about Fresh being the middle man. They're trying to connect them with a Mexican money laundering operation," Brian said, as he paced the floor.

Jade jumped from the sofa and said, "Wait a minute Brian, I have something that might help out." She went into the second bedroom where she kept her files, and brought out the pictures, Scooter had given her.

She handed them to Brian, and identified the heavy-set man as, Juan Gonzalez. She told him Tee, had identified him also, and said he was from Mexico.

Brian passed the pictures to Phillip and said, "Take a look, man." He turned back to Jade and asked, "Can I take these with me? I'll bring them back. This information will certainly be helpful."

"Sure." Jade said. "Especially, if you think it will help."

"Man, Fresh might be the link they need. All he has to do is cut a deal with the feds," Phillip said.

"Fresh has to cut a deal, what do you mean?" Jade asked.

Brian cleared his throat, then he began to explain. "This is what I wanted to tell you, Jade. Fresh is in more trouble than we originally thought. He will have to work with the feds in order to save himself.

"Like Phillip said, he could be the link they need in order to bust this operation wide – open."

Jade sat down on the sofa. She felt the uneasy feeling in her stomach, again. She wondered how Fresh would take the news. Her intentions were not meant for him to get in trouble. But – she thought, *Fresh was the one, who was breaking the law. He was going to get caught eventually. This deal is the best thing for him. He's got to go for it!*

Kim noticed Jade in deep thought. She moved closer to her on the sofa, and held her hand.

"Look, Jade. I tried to warn you about Fresh. You have nothing to feel guilty about. If anything, he needs to be thanking

you. This is a way out for him – and he'd be a fool not to accept it. It's his choice, Jade," Kim said, with compassion.

Jade smiled, and nodded in agreement.

The doorbell rang, Fresh and Tee had arrived. Jade asked them to come in, and have a seat. She introduced everybody. Fresh was skeptical about talking in front of the two detectives.

"It's okay Fresh," Jade said assuredly. "You can trust them, they're here to help you, I promise." Fresh felt a little eased. He trusted Jade.

She explained to him some things had changed, but reassured him, they were in his best interest.

As Brian and Phillip talked with Fresh about the information, they had received, Jade was on pins and needles. She watched Fresh, as they spoke to him.

"Here's the deal, and this is the good news, Fresh. Once you agree to cooperate with the feds, you sign an affidavit of fact, and your attorney can ask for grant of immunity. That will be your protection from further prosecution.

"They would probably get Lee and the others, under the Ricco law," Brian said.

"What's the Ricco law? Fresh asked.

"It's where any money is operated through illegal means," Brian explained.

"Man, this is your way out, but it's up to you. It's your decision," Phillip added.

Fresh looked pale as a ghost. Tee held onto his arm tightly. She was staring at him, while everyone awaited his decision.

He appeared tired, as he began to speak, "Okay, I'll do it. Make arrangements for me to meet with the detective, and I'll call my attorney. I'm looking forward to making a 'fresh start."

He looked at Jade, who was relieved, and said, "I knew this day would eventually come, and it wouldn't be easy. But – I have nobody to blame but myself. If it wasn't for you, Jade, I probably never would have found the courage to make these changes. Thank you, Ms. Jade."

She smiled, and gave him a hug.

Jade reiterated her plan to everybody. She wanted Fresh to let her into their office so she could get into the computer and download some files.

She wanted to find out how many loans were still active, and she wanted to see each of those files, she thought that if Lee was hiding something, she would find it on his computer.

Jade asked Fresh to get her as much information as he could regarding Lee's bank accounts.

"First, let me make a suggestion," Fresh said. "I think it would be better if Tee went with me, Jade. You know, Lee could show up at any moment. Besides, Tee has excellent computer skills."

Jade laughed and said, "I like the way you think!" Kim, Brian, and Phillip also agreed, Tee should go.

Jade asked Fresh to fill Brian and Phillip in on how things got started.

Fresh began telling them he had originally helped Lee get the business started by loaning him $250,000.

He didn't know who Lester Albright was. Lee had never mentioned him as being the previous owner, nor did he tell him that he was his father.

All Fresh knew was somebody had left this business in a financial mess. Lee was having trouble paying back the loan to

Fresh, so one day, he approached him with the idea of getting into the drug business, so he could start generating some funds quicker.

Fresh introduced him to his people, and from that point on, Lee started making enough money to take care of past debts, pay him back, and get the business off the ground.

Eventually, Lee got the big-head, and got too greedy. A lot of things started happening that Fresh didn't want any part of. Lee started to make a lot of enemies.

Fresh said he sometimes felt Lee was holding back on him, and whenever he would approach him about it, they would always end up arguing. Lee had serious attitude problems, and a short temper – which were probably the result of his heavy cocaine use.

Fresh planned to eventually get out of business with him, and go legitimate. He didn't trust Lee, and he was tired of looking over his shoulder. He told them he was doing very well with the construction and renovation business – and felt like that was all he needed.

Jade was about to wrap everything up, when she realized there was still something that she needed to address.

She looked at Phillip with compassion, and said, "Phillip, there is something else I need to find out, and if you ask me not to pursue this, I won't."

Phillip appeared anxious, but he maintained his composure, and said, "Go ahead and tell me what it is Jade.

"All I wanted to do was protect my family from any hurt, or harm. When I heard my mother tell you this morning she was all right and you should go ahead and finish what you were sent here to do – that's all I needed to hear.

"My Mother is strong in her faith, and she was feeling something this morning. Something that let me know everything is going to be all right."

They hugged each other, and Jade said to him, "Phillip, I know about Nikki, and Lester Albright. I'm sorry."

Phillip didn't speak. He nodded.

Jade continued, "Did you know Jennifer had a twin?"

Phillip was surprised, and shook his head. "No, I didn't know."

Jade said, "Well, according to Peggy, Nikki gave birth to twins. She didn't know if the other baby was a girl or boy. Since

they had been given up for adoption at birth, she didn't know what had happened to Jennifer's twin.

"Phillip, I would like to find out what happened – but I don't want to upset Mama Jo with a lot of probing questions, so I need your help."

"Okay. What do you need?" Phillip asked.

"Do you know Jennifer's birth date and the hospital where she was born?" Jade asked. "Kim knows someone who works with records who is going to try and help us find out what happened with the adoption, and hopefully the other twin."

After the initial shock of hearing what Jade had said, Phillip breathed a sigh of relief. "Maybe this is what Mama was feeling. She had been burdened down for so long with these secrets, and now she's ready to let go, ready for them to be revealed."

He then told Jade that he didn't know Jennifer's exact birth date but he knew she was born in March at Meharry Hospital, and it was in either 1975 or 76.

Tee interrupted, "Meharry Hospital? I know someone who works in medical records there. I can have her to check it out for me, if that's okay?"

Both Phillip and Jade thought that was a good idea. Tee wrote down Nikki's name, the month and year the twins were born. Then she and Fresh left to go by the office for the information Jade had asked for. They promised to get back with Jade the next day.

Phillip appeared saddened. He sat very quiet while everyone else talked.

When Kim noticed, she asked, "Are you all right sweetheart? You look like you were somewhere in the future."

She wanted to change his mood, and she had hoped that her statement would make him laugh.

It did. They all laughed, and Jade spoke up, "Phillip, everything is going to be fine. I know it is. At first I had all kinds of apprehensions about doing this story – but it was Mama Jo's inspiration that gave me the courage to continue.

"The more I found out about how ruthless and reckless Lester Albright had been to this family and others, the more determined I became to destroy his legacy, and that includes his son!"

"You go girl! That's what I'm talking about. Baby – believe it, when she says she is determined to do something, then she's ready

to kick some butt – and I got her back!" Kim said, as she stood up to give a high five to her friend, trying desperately to lift Phillip's mood.

After watching and listening to Kim's animations, Phillip couldn't help but to feel better and laugh.

He looked at Jade and said, "Jade, I – like your friend, Kim, have all the confidence in the world in you. And although I don't know all the details yet, I feel what you are trying to do, and it's all good. But you can't do it alone, Jade. We are here to help you. ***We all got your back!"***

Everyone laughed and gave high five's. Kim was glad to see Phillip's mood change. As they were preparing to leave, Kim hugged Jade and thanked her for caring about Phillip, and his family.

She told Jade to get some rest, and she would call her the next day with whatever information she was able to obtain.

Brian and Jade spent the rest of the day together listening to music and watching movies. They later went out for dinner.

The phone was ringing off the hook. Jade's hand fumbled around until she found the receiver. The noise had startled her.

She looked at the clock as she answered the telephone, "Hello," Jade said sleepily.

"Good morning sleepy head, you must have had a busy night, it's almost nine o'clock," it was Sean.

Jade replied in a groggy voice, "I know, yesterday was a busy day," she yawned. "Boy-I must have really been tired, did you get my message?"

"Yeah, that's why I'm calling. Sorry I didn't get back to you any sooner. So what's going on?" Sean asked.

Jade began to tell him all that had happened since they last spoke. She asked him not to say anything to Bob yet. She was afraid he would pull her off the story. Sean was clearly upset too, and threatened to pull her himself.

He screamed through the telephone, and asked, "Jade, are you nuts or what? That man could have killed you! He could still try and do something. This has gotten way out of hand, and it's too much for you to handle! I can't just sit back, and watch you get hurt or killed!"

Jade panicked. She knew Sean was serious – and she also knew his concerns were justified, but he didn't understand. This was something that she had to complete. She tried to calm him down, and get him to hear her. "Sean, listen – listen, Sean! Please listen to me! I understand why you are feeling this way. I know you care about me, and I appreciate that – but I've got to finish this, I'm almost there! Just trust me Sean – please trust me on this one.

"It's not like I'm working alone. I told you Brian and Phillip, who are experienced detectives, are working with Fresh and that situation. I don't have to get involved, at all.

"These detectives are professionals, they know what they are doing – and I know what I'm doing. I've put a lot of time, and effort into this investigation, just let me finish it."

Sean heard the determination in her voice, and he knew she wasn't going to give up – no matter what he said, but he would give it one more try.

"Jade, I feel the passion you have for this story, but you are losing your focus. You are trying to give back to those people what one man – who is now dead – took away. You just can't do

it. You've completed your task, you found out that Uncle Bob didn't father a child with Nikki – and that was his main concern."

"That was his main concern, Sean? Jade asked. Well, if that's the case. I guess, my mother was right. Bob doesn't care about these people."

"Jade, what are you talking about? Of course, Bob cares about what happens to the people in that community," Sean said, feeling defeated.

"If that's the case, Sean. Then, *let me to do my job!"* Jade said defiantly.

She would not be persuaded. Jade softened her voice, but her words were full of resolve, "I'm an investigative reporter Sean – and this is my job. This is what I do – and I'm supposed to feel my work. That's part of the challenge.

"You of all people should know and understand how I feel – or have you forgotten that you were once in my shoes. I told you Sean, I would never compromise my life – not even for a story.

"The incident with Lee, could have happened anywhere, I could have been running through a park, and someone could have

dragged me in the bushes – or I could have been in a parking lot, and forced into a car."

Sean felt defeated. He knew what Jade was saying was true. He once had the same determination, and fearlessness as Jade.

He decided to allow her to continue, but he made her promise to call and inform him daily of what was happening.

Jade thanked Sean for his being so understanding, and she promised him she would stay in contact daily.

Jade got up, and took a shower. She would stay around the house, so she wouldn't miss any phone calls.

It was around noon when Fresh came by to drop off a disk. He said everything she wanted was on there. He also gave her a folder with copies of bank statements, credit card charges, and receipts.

After he left, Jade began to review the disk on her computer. She had covered a lot of information, but found nothing incriminating.

Jade decided to look at his banking statements. She noticed he had several accounts in foreign banks, where he was depositing large sums of money on a regular basis.

As she was looking through the credit card receipts, the telephone rang. It was Tee.

She told Jade her friend had found the birth records of twin girls born at Meharry Hospital in March of 1975, to a Nikki Johnson – but there was no birth date indicated, nor was the adoption mentioned. The twins were born naturally, and without any birth defects, both weighed five pounds and some ounces, and their blood type was O positive.

Jade thanked her for all the information and told her how helpful it was. Jade knew Kim's friend would have a more difficult time with the adoption papers, since that kind of information is usually sealed by the courts.

As Jade sat at her computer, she thought about the information she had from Tee. She found it odd the birth dates, and information about the adoption was not present in the records, and she wondered why.

Jade also wondered why Nikki decided to keep one child – and not the other, since they both were born without any birth defects.

The most puzzling question was what had happened to the other twin.

Just then someone knocked on Jade's door, interrupting her thoughts. She got up from her computer, and went to the door, shocked to see who it was.

"May I come in?" The person asked. "I need to talk to you. There's something very important that you need to know."

Jade hesitated, then stepped back, and said, "Sure, come on in."

CHAPTER X

CONFIRMATION

Peggy Anderson appeared very nervous as she walked into Jade's apartment, and sat down. Jade asked if she could get her anything to drink, and she wanted tea.

While Jade was preparing the tea, her telephone rang. It was Kim, who said her friend was unable to find out anything on the adoption.

Jade was disappointed, but she knew it was a possibility. She told Kim Peggy Anderson had come over to tell her something important, and she would call her back later.

Jade brought two cups of tea in the living room and sat down.

Peggy began to speak. "Jade I wasn't very honest with you the other day when you came to my house."

Jade responded quickly, "I know, Peggy. I know Lee is your son, and that Lester Albright is his father. Why do you deny that?"

Peggy seemed surprised that Jade knew, but she continued to speak, "I too, like Nikki, despised Lester. I had been in the same trap as she was – only several years earlier.

"I had gotten pregnant, and trying to raise a child alone and attend school, proved to be too much. Lee had behavioral problems, and Lester felt he needed special care – so he took my son away from me, and had his sister to raise him.

"They kept him from me until he was grown. Nikki and my family were the only ones who knew about this. People who knew I was pregnant suspected something, but they really didn't know what had happened.

"Lee and I are not very close. He resents me for giving him away, and blames me for his problems. I have tried to explain to him what happened, but he won't hear it.

"I didn't want him to have anything to do with Lester's business, but he was determined to pick up where his father left off. He inherited the business.

"Lee is on drugs, and doesn't care about hurting, or using people. He can be very violent and dangerous."

Jade thought, *that's understatement,* and she decided to tell Peggy about what Lee had done to her.

"Peggy, I know first – hand what Lee can be like," then she informed her, what happened that day.

"Jade, I'm so sorry he did that to you – and that's why I'm here," Peggy said with sincerity. "I just found out Jennifer and Lee has been involved with each other."

Jade covered her mouth with both hands. She was astounded. She said, "Oh my God! I feared it was happening – but I was hoping I was wrong. You see Peggy, I just told Mama Jo and her family, Lee was Albright's son. Jennifer became very upset with me. She thought I was lying."

"I know, Jennifer told him about your conversation with her family, and that you had also been to see me," Peggy responded. "She told him, who you were, and the story you were writing about. He called and asked me to come over.

"I immediately went there, and as I reached the front door I overheard them arguing. The saddest part is, he already knew she

was his sister – and he told her so. I don't know how he knew; I've never said anything to him.

"Jennifer became so upset from hearing this, she lost it. She nearly destroyed his living room. She broke up everything in site. Jennifer was truly hurt.

"Lee was furious, and he hit her so hard in the face it knocked her down. He began chocking her.

"That's when I stopped him. It was a good thing I got there when I did, or he would have killed Jennifer. You see, Lee believed it was Jennifer who killed Lester. And in his twisted mind – this was his way of getting even with her, I guess."

"That's sick Peggy. I don't understand Lee. I mean, even if Jennifer did kill Lester, she was justified. He was an evil man who caused her mother to commit suicide," Jade said.

"Perhaps you'll understand him better once I tell you about his past," Peggy responded. "I'm trying to get in touch with his Doctor to have him committed again.

"See Jade, his aunt told me when he was younger, he constantly fought in school, and had trouble getting along with the teachers. He also exhibited hostile behavior towards girls.

"Lee would go around their neighborhood killing black cats and trying to hurt other animals. He was eventually hospitalized, and heavily medicated, but he stopped all of his medical treatments after Lester died."

Jade gasped, and said, "Peggy, I found a dead black cat on my stairs yesterday, and his throat had been slit. I had a feeling it was Lee, and I had been getting hang – up calls also, but I had no idea he was this bad off. Although, I did get bad vibes every time I was around him."

Jade was horrified, about what happened to Jennifer, and she was very disturbed about what she had just heard about Lee. Immediately she thought about what Mama Jo had said one day about Jennifer – that awful thing that happened to her.

***Could she have been talking about Jennifer killing Lester Albright,* Jade wondered?**

"Do you think Jennifer killed Albright?" she asked Peggy.

Peggy shook her head, and answered, "I don't know."

"Do you know where Jennifer is now? I need to see her," Jade said.

"She's at home, I just saw her car parked out front," Peggy responded. Then she said, "Jade, you are going to have to be careful, Lee is looking for you, and he plans to hurt you. You should call the police."

"I never should have gone in his house in the first place, that old man tried to warn me," Jade said, reflecting back.

Peggy appeared perplexed, "What old man, and he tried to warn you about what?"

"I was out running one morning, when I came upon Lee's house." Jade explained. "I knew it had belonged to Lester Albright, and so I stopped just to look at it. Out of nowhere, this little old man appeared in the yard.

"I thought he worked there as Lee's gardener, but Lee told me he took care of his own yard, but I remember the man saying that he worked there in the yard. Anyway, he kept telling me that I should leave because the house was evil, and he just kept saying that over and over and then he walked off."

Peggy was clearly shaken as she spoke, "I think I know who that was."

She quickly, changed the subject and said, "Jade, we've got to do something with Lee before he hurts you, or he gets hurt. I dislike my son's ways, but he is still my son, and I love him. I would like to see him hospitalized and getting all the help he needs."

Jade thought Lee needed more than hospitalization. *He needed to be put away for life – behind bars.*

Just then the telephone rang. It was Mama Jo, and she was hysterical.

"Jade, come help me – please! It's Jennifer!" She hung up the telephone.

Jade informed Peggy, they ran down to Mama Jo's house. Mama Jo was screaming and crying, "Please wake up, baby! Wake up! Don't leave Mama!"

She was in Jennifer's room. Jennifer was lying face up on her bed – she wasn't moving, and there was an empty prescription bottle, clutched in her hand.

As Jade ran over to the bed, and pulled Jennifer up. Her body went limp, and she was able to see her bruised face where Lee had hit her.

An overwhelming wave of emotion swelled up in Jade's body as she screamed out, and slapped each side of her cheeks, "Jennifer! Don't do this! Don't do this Jennifer! You're stronger than this! Wake up sweetheart! I am so sorry – but I had to tell you! Please wake up so that I can make it up to you!"

Peggy, who was a nurse, knew how grave the situation was – and phoned 911. She pushed Jade to the side, and began lifting Jennifer up, she began checking her air passages and taking her pulse.

Peggy asked Jade to sit on the bed and hold Jennifer up, while she tried to obtain a pulse.

Jade held Jennifer tightly against her, as if she was trying to emit life from her own body and into Jennifer's.

She cried out, "Breathe! Jennifer, breathe! Please God help me – don't let her die! Please God."

Jade felt a slight movement from Jennifer, and then she heard her groan.

She cried again, "That's a good girl! Breathe sweetheart! Breathe!"

By that time the paramedics had arrived. They grabbed Jennifer, and put her on the stretcher.

One of the attendants began asking questions, but Jade couldn't talk. She was too emotional – so Peggy explained as much as she could.

Jade hugged Mama Jo, who was sitting down at the table with her eyes closed – rocking back and forth, praying and crying.

"Lord, please don't take my baby from me! I need her Lord! She's all I got! She can't die like this – not again Lord! I lost Nikki! Please don't take away Jennifer! Please don't let it happen again!"

The paramedics said they needed to get her to the hospital, and Jade asked to ride in the ambulance. Peggy followed with Mama Jo in the car.

Jade had to sit up front, but she could see them through the window fiercely working on Jennifer. As the siren screamed through the traffic, Jade would sometimes glance out of the window but everything was blurred.

It seemed like an eternity before they reached the emergency parking lot at Vanderbilt Hospital. Jade jumped out of the front

seat, and ran along side of the stretcher with the attendants as they wheeled Jennifer through the emergency doors.

Jade looked down at her, as she lay there so bruised – so lifeless and completely unaware of her surroundings. They had put an oxygen mask over her mouth.

The nurses stopped Jade as she tried to enter the triage area. Mama Jo and Peggy came through the doors.

"Is she all right?" Mama Jo asked.

Jade grabbed her arm, as Mama Jo appeared to be losing her balance, and they sat her down in a chair.

Peggy spoke up as she patted Mama Jo on the arm, "Jennifer's going to be all right Ms. Josephine. I know she's going to make it. Now you calm down. Jade – ask the nurse for a cup of water."

Before Jade could get up, a nurse was bringing Mama Jo some water. She asked if she could get anything else.

By this time Phillip, Kevin and Brian were coming through the door. Jade had called Brian from her cell phone, in the ambulance, before they left for the hospital.

Jade ran into Brian's arms, and Phillip asked Mama Jo what had happened.

Through tears she began to tell them. "Jennifer has been upset every since Jade told us about Albright's son. I didn't even know Jennifer knew him. She had been arguing with him over the phone all last night, and this morning about something.

"Then she left the house. When she came back, she was crying. Somebody hit the chile in the face. I tried to see to her, but she wouldn't let me.

"She wouldn't even tell me who hit her. She just went in her room, and closed the door. After a while I noticed things were too quiet in there – and she wouldn't answer me, so I went in her room and that's when I found her."

Mama Jo began to cry. Kevin hit the wall and said, "If my sister dies, I will kill Lee. Matter of fact – I'm going to kill him anyway for hitting her."

Brian tried to console him, telling him that everything was going to be fine.

A Doctor came out to speak to the family. He was a large, older man with graying temples. He spoke softly, as everyone

eagerly waited to hear what he was about to say. "Hello, I'm Dr. Hamburg, and I just want to let you all know that we were able to save Jennifer. It was close, but she's going to be okay."

Everyone let out sighs of relief, and Mama Jo started crying tears of joy.

"However," he continued, "it was touch and go there for a minute – but I want to commend you all for your quick thinking and getting her here as soon as you did. I'm sorry, but she lost the baby – and she will have to undergo minor surgery."

"Lost what baby?" Kevin shouted. "Jennifer wasn't pregnant! What are you talking about?"

Dr. Hamburg continued, "She was eight weeks pregnant, but she miscarried due to the trauma her body has gone through. We need someone to sign the papers, and also give the nurse some information about her blood type. She's hemorrhaging and could possibly need a blood transfusion."

Mama Jo said, "I'll sign the papers, but I can't remember what her blood type is. Kevin can you think of it?"

Jade, who remembered Tee had just given her that information earlier said, "It's O positive."

Peggy, looking confused, chimed in and said, "No Jade, it's B positive. That's what Lee's blood type is."

Phillip looked at Peggy, and asked, "Are you Lee's Mother?"

Jade grabbed Phillip's arm and quickly explained to him why Peggy was there – and how she had helped save Jennifer.

He apologized to her, and she told him she understood.

The nurse, who had been standing there as they debated about Jennifer's blood type, said she would type her blood, and let the family know.

Phillip had called Kim earlier, and she had arrived when the doctor was talking.

She pulled Jade to the side and asked, "Are you sure that Tee said O positive?

"If that's the case. Jennifer and Lee aren't brother and sister – and you know what that means."

Jade was thinking, she was sure she had heard Tee correctly, and immediately she thought about calling Bob.

She pulled out her cell phone and dialed his number. "Hello Ms. Smith, this is Jade. Is Bob in?"

"Sure Jade. Hold on a second, please," she said. Bob picked up, shortly afterwards. "Hey Jade, what's going on?"

"I can't talk long, and I'll explain later. Could you tell me what your blood type is?"

"Bob's blood type is O positive," Jade said to Kim, and Peggy – as she clicked off her phone. "Unless Albright was an O positive, then he's not Jennifer's father. Are you sure Lee's blood type is B positive?"

Peggy pulled out a card from her wallet with American Red Cross information on it. She looked at Jade as she read it and said, "Lee's blood type is B positive."

Jade and Kim grabbed each other's hand and sort of danced around in glee – hoping Jennifer's type would come back as O positive.

"What's going on with you girls, what's this about Jennifer's blood type?" Mama Jo looking puzzled, asked.

Jade decided it was now time to talk with Mama Jo about Bob and the other child, the missing twin. She sat down in the chair next to Mama Jo, and held both of her hands.

Everyone else gathered around, and Jade began to tell her about Bob. She explained how much he had cared for Nikki, and desperately wanted to know if Jennifer was his daughter. She said if Jennifer's blood type was O positive, then she would most likely be Bob's daughter – and not Lester Albright's.

She also told her Peggy had informed her about Jennifer's twin.

Mama Jo looked somewhat relieved. She really didn't know Bob, but she was glad to hear about the possibility of him being Jennifer's father – rather than Lester Albright.

However, the mention of the twin seemed to have had a different affect on her.

Phillip had already told Kevin about the twin and he knelt down in front of his grandmother and asked, "Mama, what happened? Why did my mother want to give her children away?"

Mama Jo sighed. She tried to hold back the tears – but she couldn't. After a few minutes, she began to explain. "Your mother loved her children. But, something bad happened to her. No Kevin – no more secrets. She was raped by Lester Albright.

"Later when she found out she was pregnant, she thought for sure those babies was his. Nikki hated that man with a passion – and when she had the girls, she decided without talking to me or her father first, to put them up for adoption.

"By the time we learned of it, one of the babies was already gone. They wouldn't tell us who had her.

"Nikki had already signed the papers – and it was too late, couldn't nothing be done. I have prayed so many times for that baby, and hope that one day I'll find her.

"The next two years were rough for Nikki. She was a very good mother, but after the adoption of the other baby, she was so sorry for what she had done. She cried for that baby everyday for the rest of her life.

"She never got over that, and living with the fact she was raped by Lester Albright. Nikki couldn't handle it – and that's when she took her life. Just like Jennifer tried to do."

Peggy was standing in the background listening to Mama Jo. She had tears in her eyes and decided to make a confession, she said, "Ms. Josephine, I know what happened to the other twin." Everybody looked at her as she continued. "I was working at

Meharry Hospital at the time when Nikki delivered, and when she told Dr. Paul Bishop, she wanted to give up the babies for adoption, he called his best friend, and colleague.

"He was a young doctor who had just completed his residency there, and had accepted a job in Chicago. He and his wife were childless, she had tried many times to get pregnant, but she couldn't. So they adopted one of the twins. The hospital handled the adoption, that's why there were no papers on file."

Jade was confused as she tried to put together the words she had just heard. ***Is she saying what I think she's saying? Dr. Paul Bishop was my father's best friend. Am I supposed to be Jennifer's other twin?*** **She thought.**

Tears began streaming down Jade's cheeks. She managed to ask what was the doctor's name, who adopted the twin?

Peggy smiled at Jade and answered, "Dr. John Lewis."

"How did you know who I was?" Jade asked, confused.

"When you first walked in the hair salon that day – but even then I really wasn't sure," Peggy responded. "Then, when you and Kim came by my house to interview me, I really knew then. It

was amazing the similarities of you, Jennifer and Nikki. Your voice – and your eyes."

Jade had chills. She was speechless. She knew she was adopted, but she loved her parents so much, nothing else mattered. She never thought it was necessary to look for her real parents.

Everybody was crying, and hugging Jade. Phillip and Kevin both said they had noticed the similarities – and had even mistaken Jade for Jennifer on some occasions.

Jade stood in the middle of the floor, it appeared the room was spinning. She didn't know what she was feeling. It was as if she was on the outside, looking in. This was a surreal moment for her.

Mama Jo stood up, and with open – arms she said, as tears ran down her face, "Come here my chile. Lord have mercy! God is good – he answered my prayers!"

Jade fell into her grandmother's arms. She hugged her tightly, as she cried.

"The very first day I met you, I knew there was something special about you, Jade," Mama Jo exclaimed, as she held onto her granddaughter. "There were days I would look at you, and

see Nikki. I could hear and feel her, but I didn't know if it was my eyes and my mind playing tricks on me, or what.

"Baby, I have prayed and prayed for this day to come for so long. The Lord gave me some signs the other day. When I told you to continue your work – it was the Spirit talking, letting me know you were here, I knew it was something –but I just didn't know what."

She and Jade cried out as they hugged each other.

The nurse interrupted, she asked if everything was all right. Then she told them the results of Jennifer's blood type – and it turned out to be O positive. Everyone jumped up and cheered as if Jennifer had already come out of surgery, and was doing well.

The nurse asked who would be giving blood, and Jade stepped up and said, "I am, after all she is my twin sister."

It was then that Jade realized Bob was not only her boss, but her father as well and Sean was her first cousin.

Peggy had eased away, and left the hospital. She wanted to check on Lee.

Bob and Sean had arrived by the time Jade came back from giving blood. Kim had called and briefed them on what was going on.

When Bob and Jade saw each other, they embraced.

Bob, with tears in his eyes, stood back and looked at Jade before he spoke, "Jade, never in my wildest dreams could I have imagined that this story would have such a happy ending as this. I am ecstatic beyond belief, I have been blessed with not one – but two daughters, one of which I have had the pleasure of working with, and have admired her works and talents for a long time.

"Now that I know you are my daughter, I can say this to you Jade, I've always felt very close to you for some reason. Now I know why. I guess, as you always say, 'I was feeling you."

They laughed, and he continued. "I paid special attention to your work, naturally because it was good, but for other reasons as well. You always reminded me of my father, and the way he worked – and to be truthful, you reminded me of Nikki as well."

At that moment, Bob became filled with emotions. He could no longer speak. Jade embraced him again, reassuring him all was well.

Jade hugged Sean, and in a light-hearted moment, teased him, "Sean, now aren't you glad that you listened to my good judgment, and we never dated each other? Can you imagine how devastating it would have been if we – being first cousins – had gotten married?"

"Jade you are so right, and I hadn't even thought about it that way. But you know what, there is such a thing called '*kissing cousins,"* Sean smiled sarcastically.

They laughed as Jade playfully hit at him, and they talked a few more minutes then Jade introduced them to everyone. Bob had pulled himself together – and was elated about finally meeting Nikki's family.

Phillip shook Bob's hand. He suggested, them taking a DNA test, to be absolutely sure. Although, he felt in his heart Bob was the father. Jade and Bob agreed.

Kim hugged Jade, who was standing by Brian, holding his hand.

She, never being short on words, laughingly said, "Jade, not only were you looking at your cousin – but at your uncle as well.

When you first met Phillip, you were all goo-goo –eyed over him. Girl, what is your problem! You trying to keep it in the family!"

Everyone laughed, including the blond-headed nurse, who was assisting the family.

"No Kim. It just goes to show, I appreciate a good-looking man, when I see one," Jade shot back. She pointed to Brian, and said, "This is what I mean, and hopefully, we're not any kin!" They laughed.

Two hours had passed since Jennifer had gone into surgery. Dr. Hamburg came out a short while later, and informed them Jennifer was doing well, and they could see her in an hour.

As everyone assembled themselves onto the elevator, and headed to Jennifer's room on the ninth floor, they were all silent. Jade was apprehensive, as she contemplated Jennifer's reaction, when she finds out Jade is her twin sister.

Upon entering the room, an older, small – framed, nurse was administering medication to Jennifer.

The nurse motioned for them to come in. Jennifer stared, as they filed in, one –by – one. After the nurse left, Jade sat on the

edge of the bed and held Jennifer's hand. Mama Jo leaned over and kissed her on the forehead and asked how she was feeling.

She told Jennifer, Jade had something very important to tell her.

"What is it Jade?" Jennifer asked, in a weak voice.

Tears, once again, filled Jade's eyes as she began to speak. "Jennifer, when you were born, there was another baby born also – a girl. Nikki gave birth to twin girls, however one was given up for adoption."

With a curious look and the same frail voice, she asked, "Are you saying I have a twin sister, who is she? Where is she?

"Yes Jennifer, you have a twin sister, and I know who and where she is," Jade could not control the tears, but she continued to speak. "She's right here – I am your sister, your twin sister! I was adopted." Jade began to cry.

It was a profound and emotional moment. One, filled with happiness, tears of joy, anxiety and fears. Mama Jo was being consoled by Phillip, and Brian rushed to hold Jade.

Jennifer had tears in her eyes, but she held them. There were too many unanswered questions.

"Jade, I knew there was something strikingly familiar about you. I felt a connection, but I resisted the feeling. I am glad that you are my sister, but this is so overwhelming, and I need to know more," Jennifer said, still confused.

After Jade composed herself, she began to tell Jennifer about Bob and Nikki.

Bob and Sean went to the gift shop, and picked up some flowers and balloons for Jennifer. Everyone was still in the room when they came in. Bob walked over to Jennifer's bed, and looked down at her battered and bruised face.

With tears in his eyes, he leaned over and kissed her on the cheek, and gently rubbed her forehead. Afterwards, he showed her the beautiful floral arrangement, and then placed them on the night stand.

Jennifer was still a little groggy from the anesthesia but her eyes were filled with curiosity.

"Thank you, for the flowers, they're beautiful. Are you really my father?" She asked.

Bob, barely able to stop the tears from flowing, held her hand and replied, "Yes, sweetheart, I am your father – and I am so sorry you had to go through this. I hope you will find it in your heart to forgive me for waiting so long, and if you will allow me, I promise to make it up to you and Jade."

Bob continued to speak, "I have someone here I want you to meet. Jennifer, this is your cousin Sean. He is my nephew."

Bob stepped back as Sean came closer to the bed. He gently lifted her hand and held it as he spoke, "I've heard a lot about you Jennifer – and being Jade's twin, you've got to be an awesome girl," he leaned over and kissed her also.

Although this information was overwhelming to her, she was relieved to know she had not slept with, or had been impregnated by her brother.

Jennifer looked at her grandmother and said, "Mama, I love you! Please forgive me for what I did. I didn't mean to hurt you, I knew better, but I was in pain, and confused.

"I just didn't know what to do. Life is funny. I had resented my mother for all these years for taking the easy way out. All I could think about at the time, was how she must have felt – how

bad she was hurting – and I didn't want to hurt like that either. So I tried to do the very same thing she did. I am so sorry Mama."

"I understand baby, its okay. It's over now," Mama Jo said, smiling.

Jennifer then said to Bob, "Bob, you just don't know how happy I am to meet you and Sean – and to know that you are my real father. It's going to take some time, but soon we are all going to be one big happy family."

Bob smiled and said, "That's a bet baby girl. That's a bet."

Later on that evening, after everyone had left the hospital and went home, Jade and Mama Jo sat at the dining room table talking.

Mama Jo was elated everything had turned out okay with Jennifer. She was just as elated to have Jade, there with her. She had been singing and humming all evening long.

Jade had already called her mother to tell her what had happened, and surprisingly they were able to open up to each other and talk.

Carol Lewis was very sympathetic and understanding about what Jade had told her, yet she had some ambivalent feelings about the situation. However, she wanted her daughter to be happy, so she didn't push the issue; she informed Jade she would be flying in the next day.

As Mama Jo and Jade were talking, Jade decided to ask about Lester Albright. "Mama Jo, I have something to ask, and I hope it doesn't upset you."

"What is it Baby?" Mama Jo asked.

"Did Jennifer kill Lester Albright?" She asked.

Mama Jo was a little surprised at the question, but she decided to answer, "No, baby. Jennifer didn't do it. Your granddaddy took the pleasure of killing that old fool.

"You see, he had started eyeing after Jennifer, and one night he was drunk, and came over here wanting to take her home with him. He grabbed that chile and was about to take her out the door when Tom and me asked him to leave her alone.

"She was just a screaming and a kicking, then she pulled away and that's when Tom let him have it. Twice in the chest. Tom told

him he had hurt Nikki, but he'd die before he'd let him hurt anybody else in this family.

"It was dark outside, so Tom moved his body out of the house, and put it into Lester's car. Then he drove it down to his house, and propped him up in the front seat. That's how he was found the next day.

"Nobody ever suspected Tom, I don't imagine nobody even cared."

Jade was surprised and confused, "But didn't he think she was his daughter? Did he know?"

"Sure he knew," Mama Jo replied. "He didn't care either. That's just the kind of man he was – so he got what he deserved.

"I just hated it for Tom, cause afterwards he felt so bad about having that man's blood on his hands that he didn't do no good healthwise. On his deathbed, he asked for forgiveness as our minister prayed for him.

"Poor Jennifer was so upset about the whole incident; I think she tries really hard to blank it out of her mind. The poor chile has suffered so much, and now this has happened to her. I don't know if she'll ever be right.

"We gonna' have to press charges against Lee before he come and try to hurt ya'll again. He's just full of evil."

Jade agreed, but clearly she was preoccupied, with something Mama Jo had just said about Lee being full of evil. It reminded her of the old man she had seen in the yard that day.

She told Mama Jo about the incident, and asked if she knew who he was. She also told her when she mentioned it to Peggy, she appeared shaken, but acknowledged she knew who Jade was talking about.

"Baby, from what I hear you saying, it sounds like you described Mr. Will," Mama Jo said curiously.

"Who is Mr. Will?" Jade, equally as curious asked.

Mama Jo hesitated before responding. "He's the man who owned that property before Lester stole it from them."

Jade perplexed said, "I thought he was dead." When she saw the expression on Mama Jo's face, she knew what the answer was going to be – and an eerie feeling came over her.

"You mean, I was talking to a ghost?" Jade asked surprisingly.

"It's God's work, baby. He was just trying to warn you."

Mama Jo said.

CHAPTER XI

ALL THINGS WORK TOGETHER...

Two days had passed since the drama occurred on Montrose Avenue. Jennifer was released from the hospital and she was recovering well.

Her doctor suggested she seek some therapy. He told Bob and Mama Jo, Jennifer had suffered from a lot of traumatic experiences in her life. They may have caused some serious psychological damage, and he felt that she needed the help.

Jennifer agreed also, and Bob, who was eager to become a part of her life, began seeking out the best professional person in that field.

After Jade's mother Carol, arrived, she was introduced to Mama Jo, who instantly fell in love with her. Mama Jo saw her

as another daughter, and Carol was very pleased with meeting Mama Jo too.

Carol was also happy to meet Jennifer, and although the twins were not identical. She found the similarities between them to be amazing.

Carol filled them in on Jade as a child growing up in Chicago. As they shared stories, they found out how Jade and Jennifer's lives seemed to have paralleled each other.

Carol had named Jade after the nurse at Meharry Hospital who had helped them with the adoption, and Nikki had named Jennifer after the social worker, who had assisted her.

Mama Jo tried to get Jennifer interested in dance, and modeling – as did Carol with Jade, but neither girl showed interest. There were a number of other similarities among the twins, though they grew up in separate households, and separate cities.

Mama Jo and Carol discussed this for about an hour before Carol left to go to Jade's apartment.

Jade and her mother sat in the living room talking. Jade needed Carol to be with her at this point in her life, and she was happy to have her there.

They were able to talk like mother and daughter without the animosity and bitterness that had disrupted so many of their conversations in the past, and this made Jade feel good.

"Did you and Daddy ever get to meet Nikki?" Jade asked her mother. "How did you decide which baby to take?"

Carol rubbed her hand through Jade's hair, and placed her arm around her shoulders, "No, we weren't allowed to see her, it was against policy," Carol answered.

"Actually, we had planned to take the both of you, but Jennifer had a little jaundice and had to stay in the incubator longer. You were the more thriving twin, and since your father had a deadline to be in Chicago, we were pressed for time to leave.

The doctors felt you were the one who would be able to travel more so than Jennifer, at that time. I remember thinking it would be hard to separate the two of you, and I was very concerned about that.

“I was always afraid you would eventually find your twin sister and birth mother – especially when you decided to move to Nashville to work.

“That’s why I tried desperately to keep you in Chicago, Jade – but I realize now I was just being selfish, and I have wasted a lot of precious time trying to convince you.

“Will you please forgive me?”

“Of course I forgive you, mother,” Jade said as she hugged and kissed her.

“You were just scared of losing me, and your feelings were natural. Although I didn’t understand it then, when we spent all those times arguing, but I certainly do now – and I respect you for it.

“You are the only mother I’ve known, and I love you so much. You and daddy nurtured and raised me. You gave me love – how could I forget that?

“I didn’t know Nikki, but – I’ve always felt this peaceful and loving spirit around me – and now I believe it was her.

"I know she guided, and protected me through all of this. That's why I felt so compelled to take on this assignment. Everything worked out the way it was supposed to, Mama."

Carol nodded, and said, "I think you are right, Jade. That's just the nature of a mother's love, and one day, you'll experience the same feelings."

Just then the telephone rang.

"Hello," Jade said.

"Hello – Jade this is Peggy. I just called to say you and Jennifer will never have to worry about Lee ever harming you again, he was found dead in his car in front of his office building, last night."

Jade was shocked and asked, "What do you mean Peggy? What happened?"

Peggy sounded as if she had been crying. She continued, "Some detectives came by my house this morning to tell me Lee was dead. Someone beat him up pretty bad and shot him in the head. They left him in his car.

"Apparently he had been double crossing some people over their drugs and money – and had been doing it for some time. It looks like they caught up with him at his office.

"They beat him up so bad, his face was hardly recognizable. Then they shot him. Fresh had gone by the office to pick up some of his things, when he noticed Lee's car parked in the front of the building.

"It's something Lee never did. He always parked in the first space in the parking lot. He could see Lee sitting behind the steering wheel with his head down, so Fresh thought he had fallen asleep.

"As he came closer upon the car, he could see blood everywhere inside of it, and Lee's face was badly beaten. He immediately called the police, and tried to get in touch with me.

"I wasn't at home. I had spent the night with a friend, because I had this feeling something bad was going to happen. When I left the hospital the other day with you all, I had gone by his house to tell him about Jennifer – but he didn't care to hear it.

"He just sat there sniffing cocaine, looking crazy in the eyes. He asked me to leave. I was really concerned about him, and called his aunt to see if she could talk with him.

"After she called me back saying she had been trying to reach him all day with no luck. I went by his house but he wasn't there.

"I called and called half the night, but got no response. Now I know why. It has been like déjà vu' all over again, my son lived as his father did – and he died like he did."

Then Peggy began to cry. Jade was speechless. She didn't know what to say.

After a moment, Peggy pulled herself together and continued to speak, "My lawyer is meeting with me later today, and I've asked Fresh to meet with us also. He has agreed to take over the business – and he can have it because I don't want any part of it.

"I just wanted you and Jennifer to know you will never have to look over your shoulders or be afraid of Lee again. And Jade, in some strange way, you can now write a happy ending to your story."

Jade told Peggy how sorry she was. She even had a little sympathy for Lee. She wanted him behind bars, not dead. *I*

wonder who did this to Lee. He must have really pissed somebody off, **Jade thought.**

After Jade hung up, she immediately called Brian. She felt very nervous, and wondered if he and Phillip knew about Lee, but Brian wasn't in. She left a message for him to call her.

Jade told her mother about the phone conversation she had with Peggy, then she went downstairs to tell Jennifer, and Mama Jo.

Mama Jo was watching television, when Jade came in. She asked if Jennifer was there because she had something important to tell them. Jennifer heard Jade and walked into the den.

"What's going on baby?" Mama Jo asked.

"Guess what? Lee Anderson is dead. He was found in his car beaten and shot in the head, last night. Fresh found him, I've got to call him," Jade said anxiously.

"Oh well!" Jennifer said, smirking.

"Now Jennifer, don't be like that. Lord. The boy died just like his daddy. Who killed him Jade? Do they know?" Mama Jo asked.

"No, ma'am, they don't know yet," Jade responded.

Jade called Fresh on her cell phone, she asked him to meet her at Mama Jo's house. Phillip and Brian were coming inside the door as Jade got off her phone.

Jade informed them about Lee, but they had already heard about what happened to him from the detectives that were handling the case.

"Do they have any idea, who killed him? They don't think Fresh had anything to do with it, do they?" Jade asked.

"Nope. Fresh didn't do it. He and his attorney were talking with Joe and the feds, last night. Apparently, they asked Fresh to go by his office right after their meeting to remove his belongings. He called Joe immediately, when he found Lee. It just wasn't enough time.

"Lee was known to be dishonest in his business deals, and had double – crossed a lot of people. A lot of folks wanted to see him dead," Phillip said.

Jennifer sat down next to Jade and whispered, "I'm glad he's dead. Aren't you? He got what he deserved!" Then she hugged

Jade and went to her room. Jade was worried about Jennifer and couldn't wait for her to begin therapy.

It was later that afternoon when Tee and Fresh came by. He had just met with Peggy and her attorney. They greeted everyone as they walked into the den and sat down.

Phillip asked Fresh what happened. He couldn't wait to tell his story.

"Man, that was a trip seeing Lee slumped over in his car like that – his face all bloodied and beaten," Fresh reported. "I knew he was dead as soon as I saw his face and all that blood that was in the car. I was messed up, man. Scared as heck, and I started to run.

"I didn't know if they would be after me next or what, especially since I cut a deal with the cops. Then I thought it was best for me to call detective Thompson, so I sat in my car and used my cell phone. I didn't want to chance it going back into the building.

"I feel sorry for Ms. Peggy, but she's a strong lady. She tried so hard to change her son. But Lee was Lee. He didn't want to listen to her, or nobody else for that matter. He had messed over a lot of people, including me.

"I will be taking over the business as soon as the lawyer draws up the papers – and it's going to be straight renovations and construction.

"I'm going to forgive all the loans Lee had made with the homeowners. He was beating them out of their money anyway. My company will be legitimate, and the money in those foreign accounts, will be split among Peggy and myself.

"Lee put Peggy's name on the accounts, so it shouldn't be a problem getting it out.

"Peggy wanted me to tell you all, she is going to knock down Lee's house, and donate the land to the Waverly Park Community, in honor of the little old couple Lester Albright stole it from originally."

Fresh approached Jade and shook her hand, "I just want to thank you for helping me to make the decision I did. It could have

been me killed in my car, or the office. I was still a part of the business, you know what I mean – they didn't know.

"All I can say is thank you, girl. You were brilliant in your way of putting this all together, and you should be commended.

"There's one more thing Jade, I need to say. You also helped me to realize and appreciate more, someone who I care a lot about who is beautiful, intelligent and willing to work side by side with her man.

"I just wanted you to know there will be a wedding soon. After what happened last night, I asked Tee to marry me and she agreed."

Everyone cheered. Jade hugged and congratulated Tee, then she turned to Fresh, "You didn't need me to validate you, all I did was bring out in you what was already there, Fresh. You had to be the one willing to make a change, and I commend you for having the vision to see that – and the desire to do something about it." He hugged Jade and thanked her again.

"Mama Jo had baked a peach cobbler and everyone sat around talking, waiting for it to be served. Jennifer had come out

of her room earlier, and she sat quietly on the sofa. Jade sat down next to her.

"How do you feel, Jennifer?" Jade asked.

"I feel good. Thanks for asking," Jennifer said, as she smiled at Jade.

Jade wanted to know about Jennifer's drug use. She asked her to come outside for a moment.

Jennifer put on a jacket, and went on the porch. Jade asked point – blankly, "Jennifer are you still doing drugs?"

"Nope. I've given it up. I have no need for it anymore – and I don't need any intervention, if that's what you're thinking," Jennifer said.

"Well good for you – and guess what twin? You read my mind. I know Lee was supplying you – and now that he's gone, I just didn't want you to go out there in the streets, and deal with those criminals," Jade said with concern.

"What criminals are you talking about?" Jennifer asked slyly. "I don't know any criminals, just a few friends. People who watch your back, and take care of those who try to harm you."

Jade was puzzled and wasn't sure if she understood Jennifer correctly. "Wait a minute Jennifer – are you saying you know the people who killed Lee? Did you have something to do with that?"

Jennifer laughed, and turned to go back into the house. She looked back over her shoulder at Jade, and said, "Don't worry, Sis. I really have stopped doing drugs," She paused and smirked, *"Revenge is a better habit."*

Jade's mouth fell wide open, and as Jennifer went into the house, Brian came out and asked, "What are you girls out here in the cold, talking about?"

Jade was still in awe. She was thinking about what Jennifer had just said, but she kept quiet about it, and decided to change the subject.

"Hi Brian! What are you doing out here in the cold?" Jade asked as she wrapped her arms around his neck, and looked him in the eyes.

Brian kissed her slightly on the lips and asked, "So where do we go from here Babe?"

Jade shrugged her shoulders and responded, "I don't know, but if you lead, I will certainly follow!"

CHAPTER XII

JADE'S DEFINING MOMENT

Jade was back in her office, it had been a couple of weeks since she returned, and she missed being there.

The past two weeks had been very busy for her; she was feverishly working and trying to get her story out. Though, today she was beaming.

As she sat back in her chair, she couldn't help but smile when she picked up the morning edition of the *Gazette* from her desk. There it was, the first installment series on the front page, in bold print.

***Predatory Lending Operations – lend practice to money laundering, drugs, and murder,* by Jade Lewis. Also featured was one of Scooter's award – winning pictures of a house being renovated.**

"Congratulations Jade," a voice resonating from behind the paper said. She laid the paper down to see who it was. Sean, was standing in the doorway of her office.

Jade had been receiving congratulations all morning from her colleagues, including Bob, who had called earlier.

"Great Story! You pulled it off kid. How does it feel to have an award – winning investigative series?" Sean asked, excitedly.

"It feels good Sean, it really does. For a while there, I didn't know which way I was going with this story. But I'm resilient, I bounce back. You can't stop the *Jade,*" she said laughing.

"How well do I know. Remember, I'm the one who told you this assignment would spark your *creative talents,"* Sean said, as he was headed for the door.

"Thank you, Sean. I appreciate that," Jade said sincerely.

Sean stood in the doorway with his arms crossed and said, "Oh by the way, you never mentioned who you thought killed Lester Albright and Lee Anderson."

"I didn't intend to Sean. It's a mystery," Jade said with conviction.

"You know who did it, don't you?" He asked.

Jade picked the newspaper up from her desk and swerved around in her chair. With her back towards Sean, she responded, "I'll never tell!"

Sean smiled, and shook his head as he turned, and walked out the door.

Later that afternoon, as Jade sat at her desk, she began to reflect on the comment Jennifer made to her on Mama Jo's porch, *'Revenge is a better habit'*. For the past two weeks, this remark has haunted her.

What did she mean by making that statement?

Was Jennifer friends with Juan Gonzalez?

The police seem to think, he killed Lee. He has disappeared, and hasn't been seen lately.

Could Jennifer have warned him about the FBI?

Did he kill Lee because of what he did to Jennifer, or was it because Lee had swindled him?

These thoughts ripped through Jade's mind, but she shrugged them off. *Some things are best left alone,* she thought.

Jade laughed to herself, as she picked up the newspaper again. She was proud of her story, and the work she put into it. She had accomplished what she set out to do. This *was* her defining moment.

She destroyed the legacy of Lester Albright and Lee Anderson, it exists no more.

Jade began to read an excerpt from her story, 'And the Waverly Park community is recapturing its glory. It is no longer held in bondage by misrepresentation of contracts, loans, fraud, and scams. It is becoming a vibrant and thriving community, once again.'

Jade smiled and thought, they meant evil against a lot of people, but God meant it for good in order to bring about the present results.

Families found each other. Love found love, and people came together.

Jade closed her newspaper, and folded it in half. She placed it under her arm as she grabbed her purse and keys. She walked to the door, turned off the lights, and left her office.

Jade was on her way to a well-deserved, and welcomed, two – week vacation in the Caribbean, with Brian.

ABOUT THE AUTHOR

Rhonda Braden was born in Nashville, Tennessee. She has one daughter, and is married to Ronald Braden. They currently live in Frankfort, Kentucky.

Rhonda is a graduate from Tennessee State University, and has a B.S. degree in Criminal Justice.

She worked as a Social Service Coordinator, for the Metropolitan Development and Housing Agency, in Nashville, for twenty-four years. She is now a house-wife.

Rhonda is embarking on a second career: *writing* – her first love. Her genre is writing fictional novels.

She is a first-time author of the new fictional mystery/romance, novel – Montrose – and is presently working on her second novel.

Printed in the United States
857200001B